The Vision

A Novel

LORI FIELDS

BALBOA PRESS
A DIVISION OF HAY HOUSE

Copyright © 2012 Lori L Fields

All rights reserved. No part of this book may be used or reproduced by any means, graphic, electronic, or mechanical, including photocopying, recording, taping or by any information storage retrieval system without the written permission of the publisher except in the case of brief quotations embodied in critical articles and reviews.

ISBN: 978-1-4525-6327-5 (sc)
ISBN: 978-1-4525-6329-9 (hc)
ISBN: 978-1-4525-6328-2 (e)

Library of Congress Control Number: 2012921512

Balboa Press books may be ordered through booksellers or by contacting:

Balboa Press
A Division of Hay House
1663 Liberty Drive
Bloomington, IN 47403
www.balboapress.com
1-(877) 407-4847

Because of the dynamic nature of the Internet, any web addresses or links contained in this book may have changed since publication and may no longer be valid. The views expressed in this work are solely those of the author and do not necessarily reflect the views of the publisher, and the publisher hereby disclaims any responsibility for them.

The author of this book does not dispense medical advice or prescribe the use of any technique as a form of treatment for physical, emotional, or medical problems without the advice of a physician, either directly or indirectly. The intent of the author is only to offer information of a general nature to help you in your quest for emotional and spiritual well-being. In the event you use any of the information in this book for yourself, which is your constitutional right, the author and the publisher assume no responsibility for your actions.

Any people depicted in stock imagery provided by Thinkstock are models, and such images are being used for illustrative purposes only.
Certain stock imagery © Thinkstock.

Printed in the United States of America

Balboa Press rev. date: 11/19/2012

Lori Fields
Coquitlam 2024

This story is dedicated to Rachael, whose spirit and lessons live on.

Chapter 1

Janet

"Please, please, let me make it to the other side of the bridge." Janet gripped the bus strap so hard, her knuckles turned white. The bus was heaving, as usual, on a Monday morning 7:30 commute to downtown Vancouver. Janet had to stand, which she hated, because it made her feel ungrounded somehow and vulnerable. She could feel the panic attack rise up in her and inhaled shallowly, as if she couldn't get the next breath. "I have to get off this bus," she thought to herself.

Mercifully, the bus approached the end of the bridge and started down the causeway. She could feel herself relaxing slightly, but the panic was still present. Janet rang the bell and got off at the first stop after the causeway. Her knees almost buckled as she stepped off the last step of the bus. "What is wrong with me?"

She sat down on the first bench she approached and began inhaling deeply and fully, like her therapist had suggested. "Why couldn't I do that on the bus?" Janet reproached herself.

She had nearly ten blocks to walk to her office in three-inch heels, and she could feel blisters forming already from her new shoes. It was still early—she didn't need to work until nine—so she had an hour. Janet knew she couldn't take the bus, but she was still shaky and couldn't walk just yet. She turned herself around and saw the lagoon. There were some swans and ducks in there and it looked peaceful. Janet got up and walked towards it. She had always loved the water, any body of water—lakes, oceans, rivers, even ponds. Water made her feel at ease. Her anxiety dissipated when she was near it. That was one of the reasons she stayed on the West Coast, so that she would be surrounded by it.

Janet sighed deeply. She had made such progress lately, by getting a new job, joining a yoga class, eating sensibly—not bingeing or purging—and even thinking about online dating. She knew there was no way she could drive across the bridge to work, but she could take the bus. It was just that damn bridge and the fact that she couldn't get a seat. She'd thought that the earlier she went, the better the chance she would have to get a seat. But she'd had to stand up and let the old lady have a seat. She could just see the faces of everyone on the bus if she said, "Sorry, dear, but you can't have my seat, because I suffer from panic attacks." Meanwhile, the old dear is nearly breaking her legs trying to stay in one spot on the bus.

Janet's feet were killing her. "I need a pair of runners right now." Her gaze went to the underside of a bush about a foot away. To her amazement, there was a pair of pink and white running shoes. Nothing to shout about, but fairly clean and decent. "Wow," she said aloud, "I can't believe it." She went and picked them up to examine them further. They didn't smell and there looked to be new insoles inside them. She put her foot in one of them and miraculously it fit. She felt like Dorothy putting on the red shoes for the first time.

"I will only borrow them; I will bring them back," she promised. For a fleeting moment, Janet thought about what she might catch from these shoes, but it somehow didn't seem to matter. She decided to have a bit of a walk before heading to the office. There weren't a lot of people around and she felt invigorated by the cool air. Amazingly, her thoughts were kind and not recriminating as they usually were when she messed up. "I will try again tomorrow," she promised herself and felt better about the situation already.

There was a clearing off to the right of the path and, for some reason, she entered it. It wasn't exactly a marked path but it was accessible and fairly clear. She carried on walking about a hundred yards, and there seemed to be an altar of some kind, just ahead. Someone had put some stones on top of it and flowers. Janet went closer and touched the top of it. There was a breeze that came up and she felt something behind her, so she turned around. There was nothing there but when she turned back, she couldn't believe what her eyes saw. Just above the altar was a white light so dazzling that she had to adjust her focus. There was an outline of woman, fully covered. The face was visible—it was soft, ageless and incredibly beautiful. But this was not the beauty you see in fashion magazines, but rather the beauty of a landscape, a painting, a sculpture or a dance.

"Where did you come from and who are you?" Janet asked. There was a halo of golden light around the woman's head, and she was holding a crucifix.

"My God, I mean, holy shit . . . sorry, but you're the Mother Mary . . ." Janet felt the need to kneel before the apparition, but she couldn't bow her head. She had to look at her, almost drink in her loveliness. Her heart felt like it was growing bigger to hold all the love that was coming into it from this vision.

The vision didn't speak or move, only smiled. It was so powerful that Janet remained transfixed for what seemed like hours. Then as quickly as it had appeared, the vision faded away. Janet got up off her knees and brushed the dirt from her stockings. Her legs trembled as she stood up and spoke aloud. "What the heck happened just now?"

She turned around, embarrassed by her actions, hoping no one saw her. She ran along the path back to the main walkway. She looked at her watch and it was 8:30—she had half an hour to get to work. She took off the runners, placed them back where they originated and put her own shoes back on. Her high heels felt as comfortable as the runners, and she was amazed at how easy it was to walk in them. Janet didn't have time to think about what had just occurred and what she had seen, but she was filled with a sense of well-being. She started up the long trek to her office and felt like she was "walking on water."

Chapter 2

James

James toyed with the idea of skipping class but his parents would go ballistic. He was already failing math and science, and they had threatened to take away his computer if he didn't pull up his grades. Big joke, his parents—they were separating for a while but "trying to work things out"—yeah, they had divorce written all over themselves.

James was walking through the park; he didn't want to hang out at school during lunch hour. The park made him feel better, unlike everything else in his life. School was crap. He was mad at his friends because they were being stupid about, about . . . well, just being stupid. His younger sister had some kind of autoimmune condition he couldn't understand, let alone pronounce, and his face was full of zits. The only thing that made him feel better was smoking some pot. It was no big deal and didn't hurt anyone. He wished he had a joint on him now. He didn't even want to listen to his iPod. "God, my life sucks," James said out loud. He cut through to a path he normally didn't use, but today he felt compelled to walk along it. Up ahead he could see a bright light. "Oh shit, is it the cops?" Thankfully, he didn't have a joint on him. James was curious, so he walked towards the light.

"They must be filming some kind of movie or TV show," James thought. He approached the lighted area tentatively. He could see an altar up ahead and immediately thought of some kind of "goth freak show." James had a hard time understanding what it meant and why anyone would want to dress up like they are vampires or the dead. "Man, they are some weird dudes."

As he approached the altar, the light became brighter and he thought he could see a woman standing in the light. "What the fuck is that?" Strangely, James wanted to go closer. He inched his way towards the apparition. He could clearly see what looked like an angel at first, but then he didn't see any wings. The woman wore a long flowing gown and roses lay at her feet. Instinctively, James wanted to run away but he was frozen to the spot. He began to feel calmer and more at ease as he continued to look at her. His whole body relaxed and he felt like he did when he toked up. She smiled at him and held her hands out as a gesture of love.

"I don't know who you are, lady, but I need to keep looking at you." For what seemed like hours, James stayed riveted to the spot. Gently, almost like a sunset, the apparition started to fade and then diminished altogether. James began breathing rapidly, as he felt like he had been holding his breath. He looked at his watch: 12:45. He had only been there about 30 minutes. It seemed way longer than that. He knew he had to get back to school. James began the walk through the park. He didn't know what had happened but he felt lighter, like someone had taken a load off him. He also felt the urge to run back to school. "Man, what a trip," he said as he jogged back.

Chapter 3

Jacob

Jacob's whole body ached as he walked through the park with his cane. "My doctor said I have to keep active. Sure, he would say that because he doesn't have an arthritic body like mine. Let him walk in my shoes," Jacob muttered to himself.

Every morning for the past year, Jacob had walked a portion of the park to get the exercise his doctor subscribed to. He even followed this regime when it rained, but not in the snow, which was too dangerous. Sadly, there was no snow this year but lots of rain. "What do you expect in a rainforest?" Jacob would often say. "Maybe I need to move to Osoyoos, where it is warmer, or better yet Florida." His brother Al lived there and was always bragging about how good the weather was.

Jacob was born in the States but immigrated in the early '50s to Vancouver for work. Here he met his beautiful wife, Lorraine. Sadly, Lorraine had died two years ago and he was left on his own. They had no children. Jacob struggled with life, even when he'd had Lorraine beside him. He seemed to be always fighting something—his work, his distant family,

Lorraine's family and mostly himself. Jacob felt a huge amount of guilt that Lorraine had died and he was still here. She loved life and was the most positive person he had ever met. "Why did God have to take her, why not me?" he would often ask himself. The only reason he did not give up on life was his promise to Lorraine that he would forge ahead, no matter what.

"Lorraine, why did you make me promise something I don't know if I can do?" Jacob would sit before her picture and talk to her at night. "I have aches and pains. I have a hole in my heart since you left me. I just don't know if I can do this..."

However, every morning he got up and had his oatmeal and the multitude of tablets his doctor prescribed for him. Simone, his care-aide, would come in at 9:00 a.m. every morning to make sure Jacob was okay and to give him a shave and prepare his cocktail of drugs and favourite "Metamucil martini." Jacob didn't feel that he needed anyone to come in and look after him, as they had a townhouse with all the maintenance looked after by the council, but it was one of Lorraine's requests that he do so. "I am still being henpecked beyond the grave," he would lament to Lorraine's picture. "I should be allowed to stay in my pajamas all day and watch TV, not get up like I have something to live for."

Simone would do a bit of light housework, while Jacob did his crossword puzzle and read the daily paper. She would prepare a light lunch and make a stew or casserole for his dinner. Jacob then went for his daily walk after lunch and Simone would leave for the day. Once he got going, he started to enjoy the fresh air and the noises of the ducks and various birds, but he would never admit it to anyone, let alone himself. The park seemed deserted this afternoon and this made him feel lonely. Despite what Jacob thought he wanted (to be left alone), he liked to have people around him—not to talk to, but as a steady presence. He saw a path that seemed to be trampled on of late and, although it wasn't paved, it was pretty clear and flat. He walked along it.

He came upon an altar. Jacob stood a fair distance away from it and was about to turn around and leave when he smelled the waft of fragrance, Lorraine's fragrance. He moved closer to the altar and bent over to smell the flowers on it, thinking that these might be the source of the fragrance. The altar suddenly lit up and a vision came into view. Jacob could see a woman clearly and reached up with his cane to see if he could touch the apparition. The cane became hot to the touch and he dropped it. To his surprise, Jacob was able to stand up without the cane's support. The woman in the vision smiled at Jacob and held her crucifix to her chest.

"I know who you are," Jacob said, "but do you know I am Jewish? I am not supposed to believe in you." Jacob shook his head as if to banish the vision, but it persisted. "What did Simone give me this morning? Some kind of drug?" Jacob looked at the apparition, perplexed. "Shouldn't you be in Lourdes or somewhere like that? What are you doing in Stanley Park? And why are you before me? I know, this is Lorraine's doing. She was Catholic, and she never did understand what it was like to be Jewish. I am not a practising Jew, you understand, but fourth-generation Jewish, so that must count for something. I think maybe you got your person mixed up. Maybe the person you were supposed to show yourself to was sick or something, and I came into the wrong path. I am always showing up where I am not wanted, so I will just leave now and you can get back to whatever it is you need to do."

Jacob felt that he needed to pick up his cane and walk away, but he didn't want to. In fact, he couldn't. He just stood there. "Well, I guess I am staying here for a while . . . hope that is okay. Do you see Lorraine at all? She was really a saint, you know. I am sure you must have bumped into her somewhere up there. Can you tell her I miss her and I am so sorry that it wasn't me that was taken? It is so unfair that she had to die and I had to stay." Tears began rolling down his face and he felt a gentle hand brushing them aside. He immediately stopped crying and looked up at the apparition. He felt a love that he had never felt before, not a love like Lorraine's love but a love for himself. He felt a kindness and a knowledge that he was worth something. It made him see, for the first time, that he was important and worth caring about.

The light began to fade and the fragrance wafted away. Jacob found himself alone once more. He picked up his cane without any effort and started back along the path. His body seemed stronger. There was not the jarring pain when he walked and, for the first time in his life, he was speechless.

Chapter 4

Janet

Janet had not been back to the place where she saw the vision. She had thought about it a lot, and had every intention of going back there, but somehow never made it. She convinced herself that she didn't need to go because she felt so much stronger, happier and safer. There was also this worry in the back of her mind that it wouldn't be there again and perhaps she had made it all up! Janet did not have the courage to tell anyone what she saw and a small part of her wanted to keep the vision for herself. Janet knew undeniably that the vision was the Virgin Mary, or Mother Mary, whatever the correct terminology was. She was not religious but all through her childhood there was a pull towards something greater than herself, something greater than everyone; it kept her going through all her dark days. Janet had been adopted when she was a baby. Despite never being told she was adopted, she somehow knew. Her first recollection was at age five when she told her mother that she knew she wasn't her "real little girl," that she was "borrowed" from her real mom; she remembered the strange look on her mother's face when she declared this. All through her life she felt "borrowed" and not belonging. Janet felt that this made her connection to God so much stronger, and although she did not belong in her family, she did belong to God.

It really wasn't a surprise to her that her family (mother, father and their biological son) moved to a different province when she was 20. They didn't seem to intentionally disown her but they wanted to put as much distance as they could between them and her. She wasn't a bad daughter, just a disappointment. Janet had a lot of phobias and insecurities that they found hard to deal with, especially as they were so secure in themselves and their own being. They didn't understand how someone that they brought up could be so vulnerable and afraid of almost everything.

Janet finished high school at the Lucas centre (night school), because she had so many panic attacks at high school, she just couldn't go there anymore after grade 10. She was intelligent and even got a scholarship when she did graduate. Unfortunately, she couldn't use it. There was no way she was going to go to university or college. Her parents left her with some financial security and even rented her an apartment. Janet knew this wasn't going to last forever and she didn't feel entitled to a free ride anyway. With the help of a good therapist, Janet made a move into the working world. She got a job as a receptionist in a small leasing firm and became a valuable employee for the company. Due to the economic times, however, the business folded after three years and Janet became unemployed.

She then started working in a temping agency and got work at various offices for another year, but the changing offices every few weeks made her panic attacks come back with a vengeance, and she had to quit. Then came the roller-coaster ride of eating disorders. Janet met a guy through one of her temping jobs. He was a salesman and a real charmer. He was also a lot older than Janet. They went out for a couple of dates and he wanted to go to bed with her. Janet was still a virgin and very afraid of "the whole sex thing." She knew that if she didn't go to bed with him, he would not want to go out with her. So Janet lost her virginity to him but, sadly, he was not a patient lover. He berated her lack of sexual knowledge and her uptight-ness.

Janet was an average weight but Mike told her she needed to lose a few pounds. She began to exercise excessively and starve herself. When she did eat, she overate and felt a self-loathing. Then began the use of laxatives and the cycle of starving-exercise, overeating-laxative use and on and on. Mike would often tell Janet that he had other women who were attracted to him and she needed to "smarten up" or he would leave her. Part of the problem was that Janet had not gone back to work. She would obsess in her apartment all day, waiting for Mike to call.

Eventually Mike left her for someone else. She found out later that he had been seeing this other woman while still going out with her. She was filled with grief and self-hatred. "I must be the ugliest loser around." Janet's self-esteem dipped to an all-time low. One morning when she went out for her jog, she saw Mike and his girlfriend. Janet had never seen her before. When he broke it off with Janet, Mike said that his new girlfriend was gorgeous and skinny. Janet couldn't believe it. This "gorgeous, skinny woman" was twice as big as Janet and even older than Mike. She was no supermodel, that was for sure. Janet felt humiliated and used.

She realized that all this self-abuse was getting her nowhere. She went back to her therapist and got herself into a better space. Janet found coping mechanisms that mostly worked for her. This last year was better and she found this wonderful job as a receptionist in a property management company, downtown. It was all falling into place, until she received a letter from the ministry saying that her biological mother was asking to meet her. Her solid world began crashing down, the panic attacks started again, and she alternated between being agoraphobic and then claustrophobic. No space seemed safe for her. Her anti-anxiety meds had been increased to help her cope. Her therapist suggested trying yoga to keep her grounded and relaxed. It, along with the breathing techniques, certainly helped her.

Since her encounter with the vision, Janet had felt calm and at peace. But her serenity was starting to diminish as she felt pressured into making a decision about whether or not to see her biological mother.

Janet was on the bus to work and she felt the jerking motion of the bus as it struggled along the causeway. There was clearly a problem with the bus. Miraculously, it made it to the first bus stop after the causeway and then abruptly stopped. The bus driver cursed and turned around to his passengers. "Sorry, folks, but it looks like this bus is not going anywhere. You will have to wait for the next one." Groans by disgruntled commuters met with, "I know, I'm sorry, but what can I do? Everyone off the bus please."

As they piled out of the bus, Janet knew where she had to go. Most people milled around the bus stop and a few started walking to their places of business. Janet immediately walked towards the park. She saw the pair of runners under the bush, looking exactly as she had left them, no better and no worse. She slipped them on, as this seemed to be part of the ritual. With purpose, Janet found the trail she had walked before and stood before the altar. She knelt before it and closed her eyes. "Please, Mother Mary, show yourself to me again. I really need to see you . . ." There was the breeze again and the light shone above the altar as it had done before. She came and smiled down at Janet. Simultaneously, Janet felt relief, gratitude and peace.

Chapter 5

James

James was not in a good space at the moment. He had tried out for the intermediate basketball team and didn't make it. He didn't even get on the reserves. James didn't understand this. He was great at basketball. He loved to shoot hoops every weekend and was one of the best players on the junior team. He seemed to have stopped growing this last year and was more uncoordinated than usual. One of his buddies suggested that it was all the pot he was smoking—it stunted his growth and did something to his brain cells. "What does he know? Just 'cause he's a jock and a goody two-shoes."

It did make James think, though. Maybe he should cut down, but it just made him feel better. On the other hand, he hadn't touched a joint since he'd seen the apparition. He just felt he didn't need to. He hadn't really analysed what it was that he saw but he knew it was something special. James wasn't even sure he wanted to see it again—it freaked him out a bit. It was like talking to a hot girl. He really liked it when he was in a hot girl's presence and had a conversation with her, but to actually try to do it again was terrifying.

James felt like such a loser. A couple of his friends had made the team and the others hadn't even tried out. He had a hard time being in their company. They either looked at him pityingly or they wondered why he had even bothered to try out. "Fuck it, who cares anyway?" James decided to go for a walk through the park after lunch. He had PE this afternoon but couldn't make himself go. He felt tired and defeated. The last few days he wished he had his sister's condition. It would be a good excuse to not go to school or even try. Then he felt bad about his sister having her illness. "Why didn't I get it instead of her? She has all the brains; it just isn't fair."

James kicked some stones ahead of him. He wished he could just shut off his brain sometimes; it made his head hurt, all this thinking about stuff. He saw the path he had taken that day and, without thinking about it, followed it again. He could see the altar ahead of him. It looked very ordinary. "See, nothing is there." James went up to the altar and threw one of the stones at it. He felt angry, like he wanted to destroy the altar and everything it represented. He raised his fist to it and then he stopped in mid-air. An overwhelming sadness came over him and he started to cry. Really cry, with gut-wrenching sobs that shook his whole body. James slumped down in front of the altar with his head in his hands. He could feel more than see the light above him. It was as though a warm blanket had covered him up. James stopped sobbing and looked above the altar. There she was in all her glory. She looked at him with such love and compassion. She didn't need to say anything but James knew she was on his side.

"Why do you want to be with me?" he asked her, but she only smiled and held her hands out to him. James stood up and bowed his head. He felt like praying. He hadn't prayed since he was about six years old. He used to do it every night before going to bed. He was not even sure when or why he stopped, but he had. James asked for his sister to get well and for his parents to get back together. He then felt calm and knew that his prayers were being listened to. Someone was listening to him and cared about what he wanted. That was all he wanted—someone to at least listen to him like it mattered. "Thank you," James whispered. The apparition faded and James was once again left alone. Strangely, he didn't feel alone; he felt part of something, something way bigger than his own little world.

Chapter 6

Jacob

Jacob couldn't believe how much better he felt since seeing the vision. He not only felt stronger physically but also emotionally. He had a long talk with Lorraine the evening after he saw the Mother Mary. "You know, Lorraine, I never really thought about someone being up there." He pointed to the ceiling. "Of course I believe in God; my own mother would have been mortified if I didn't, but other beings . . . not really, and now after seeing her, well, it does my heart good. I know you had something to do with it, so thank you, sweetheart." Jacob kissed the picture.

Jacob didn't have any desire to go back to the park, at least not yet. However, he thought and thought about what a difference his encounter there had made to his being still here on this earth. Why was he here and not Lorraine? He felt he was wasting his days just being alone in his apartment. He needed to go out and meet some people, but where? Jacob immediately thought of the seniors' centre that Lorraine used to go to. Jacob always felt it was a waste of time, but Lorraine loved it. She would go every Tuesday and Friday. They had bingo, teas, and other activities like shuffleboard.

Jacob decided he was going to join and he did the very next day. He realized that his social skills were pretty archaic and he would need to have patience with people and himself. He decided to go to bingo once a week and he even played shuffleboard. There was a couple that spoke to Jacob and made him feel at ease. They remembered Lorraine and were sad when they realized she had passed away. "She was a wonderful lady," Frank said, "very kind and outgoing." His wife Judith agreed. "She was always available to help clean up in the kitchen, even when it wasn't her turn."

Jacob would sit next to them at the teas and couldn't help wonder what it would have been like if he had gone with Lorraine. He began to feel guilty and ashamed of his ignorant behaviour. Jacob began to take stock of his life and felt more and more depressed about his inability to be flexible. Lorraine had done all the bending. When Lorraine found out she had to have a hysterectomy at an early age and this prevented them from having children, Jacob would not dream of adopting. They argued about it for a while and eventually Lorraine stopped talking about it. Jacob knew deep down that, by not allowing them to adopt, he was somehow punishing her for their inability to have children. When Jacob admitted this to himself, he cried and couldn't speak to Lorraine's picture that night. He felt like a bully. He had bullied Lorraine in many ways and now finally felt remorse.

It was becoming clear that he needed to see the vision again. His heart was breaking with guilt and shame. Two weeks to the day that he had walked through the park to the altar, Jacob again made the trip to the secluded path. It was pouring out. The heavens seemed to be crying with Jacob. When he got to the altar, he could see the stones and the flowers as they were two weeks before. There was no light or smell like last time and Jacob thought maybe she had gone. "Well, I guess you opened my eyes to what a jerk I have been. I feel terrible. I am so ashamed of the way I behaved with Lorraine. There are so many things I wish I could redo. I really don't know why Lorraine stayed with me. She probably felt sorry for me and, being the angel that she was, couldn't leave me. I am truly sorry, Lorraine, and God and Mary, I am not the man I could have been . . . should have been. I—"

Jacob stopped in mid-sentence as he suddenly smelled the fragrance once more and saw the light come from the altar. There she was in all her glory, smiling down at Jacob and holding her hands out as if to say, "You are forgiven." Jacob bowed his head slightly and thanked her. His heart felt healed and he no longer felt the heaviness he had just moments ago. "I'm not sure what you do but if you could bottle it, you would make a fortune." Jacob smiled once more and watched as the light faded and his favourite smell vanished.

Chapter 7

Janet

What they (whoever they are) say is true: You don't know what you've got till it's gone. Janet strongly felt that this morning. She had been feeling disconnected from her work and picking up some negative energy from its surroundings. She just knew there was something up. Tom, her overseeing manager, called her into his office.

"Janet, there is no easy way to say this, but we have to lay you off." Janet had felt this coming but tried so hard to ignore it and hope that it would go away. "Due to the recession, the economy, we are not getting the contracts we need to afford some staff members. The company has had to downsize . . ."

Janet stopped listening. She had to hold on tight to stop the dizziness. She felt like she was being swallowed up by the room, as if it were some terrestrial monster eating her whole.

". . . You of course can collect EI for a while and I am sure with your work ethic and skills you will find something soon. We will give you a very positive recommendation . . . Are you okay?" Tom looked at her with concern.

"Yes, it is just a shock, um, I'm sorry, but I have to go . . ." Janet almost ran from the office and into the ladies washroom. She went into one of the cubicles and locked the door. She sat on the toilet seat and put her head between her knees. She felt like she was going to pass out. "Breathe, breathe," she told herself. "Mother Mary, help me . . ." Gradually, she calmed and her breath became normal. Someone had come into the washroom. "Are you okay, Janet? Tom asked me to check on you," one of the office workers called out.

"Yes, I'm fine. I just felt a bit sick, but I'm okay."

"Are you sure? Do you want some water or anything?"

"No, no, it's okay, I'll be fine. Just give me a few minutes and I will be back at my desk."

"Okay, if you are sure . . ." The office worker left. Janet stood up. She felt shaky but stable. The perspiration on the back of her neck was sticky and warm; however, Janet felt chilled. She opened the cubicle and ran water over her face. She felt better and stronger. Just by asking for help from Mother Mary, Janet felt safe and in control.

Chapter 8

James

James couldn't get out of bed. He felt so tired and depressed. His whole body ached. He told his mom he couldn't go to school because he was sick; he had the flu or something. She didn't believe him but after she took a look at him, she decided he wasn't faking. His mom had to be at the hospital by nine. His sister had been in hospital since last week. She had trouble breathing and couldn't eat. James' mom had to meet with the doctors to discuss what would happen next, as far as treatment was concerned. "I'll call the school. Stay in bed and rest. Have some soup for lunch, and I will see you sometime this afternoon, okay?" His mom leaned over James and almost kissed his cheek but thought better of it and ruffled his hair instead.

James heard the door shut and he pulled the covers off. He felt hot and then cold and pulled the covers back over. He went over the conversation he had overheard his mom and dad having just after his sister went into the hospital.

"Karen, this is not going to get better, you know that, right?"

"Stop it, Kevin, I don't want to hear it. I can't hear it right now." James could hear his mom crying softly.

"We have to face this. Diana may not recover this time; we have gone through this before and, each time, it weakens her system and she can't fight back. Karen, this is killing me too. I can't always be the tough one. Don't you think I want to break down as well? For Christ's sake, she is my daughter too." James could hear his dad getting choked up as well.

James stopped listening after that. His sister had been in and out of hospital so many times in her short life that he thought this was just another episode. He hadn't even gone in to see her this time. His mom freaked out at him about it, but he lied and said he felt like he was coming down with something and didn't want to pass any germs on to her. This shut his mom up. She was such a germaphobe around his sister, but who wouldn't be? Now that he'd justified it by staying home from school, his mom would get off his case about seeing her.

"I'm just a wimp," James said out loud. What if this was the last time he saw his sister, what if she died? . . . James angrily threw the covers off and went into the shower. He knew where he needed to go and it wasn't to the hospital.

Chapter 9

Jacob

Jacob was not the same man he was two months ago. He was kinder, softer, gentler and, well, happier. Sometimes he would feel a bit guilty about his newfound happiness, but mostly he revelled in it. His care-aide, Simone, wanted to know what wonder drug he was taking. "You are not taking Viagra or something and have some woman I don't know about?"

Jacob laughed but he could see Simone was serious. "Shame on you, Simone. I would never go with another woman. Lorraine was my everything and I could never do that." Simone just shook her head and wondered what had gone on to change Jacob's personality.

Jacob smiled a mischievous smile and went back to his crossword. He compared himself to Scrooge and how he changed after having visitations from the three ghosts. He chuckled to himself and Simone gave him a funny look. "Are you sure you don't need a checkup or something?"

"No, no, I am fine; I am wonderful, in fact. Just be glad for me. You can take the morning off, and I will still pay you. I am going to eat at the seniors' centre anyway."

"Jacob, I don't know about this, you are so different . . ." Simone looked at Jacob and sighed. "Okay, but don't make a habit of this, I need to earn my money."

Jacob got up and went over to Simone. He held her hands and looked her squarely in the face. "I never realized how lovely you are. You are a good woman and have helped me since Lorraine died. You have put up with my crankiness and moodiness. For that, I thank you, and you deserve to have some time-off-with-pay, so go and do something for yourself."

Simone's eyes welled up and she hugged Jacob. Without saying anything, she got her purse and left.

"I have some free time now; I think I will go visit my friend." Jacob happily got his cane and set off for the park.

Chapter 10

The Meeting

Jacob hummed as he walked towards the path that he had been frequenting of late. "When was the last time I hummed or whistled," he said aloud and chuckled. He saw the familiar altar and smiled. "I am here again, dear friend." Off to one side, there was a patio chair. It had been put there for someone to sit on, obviously, and oddly enough it didn't look out of place.

Suddenly Jacob felt weary. "Too much merriment—it can't sustain a person forever. I should have had lunch before I ventured out," he mused. Jacob sat on the chair and closed his eyes.

Janet walked up along the path, almost silently in her pink and white running shoes. She saw the altar and gave a sigh of relief that it was still there. Jacob stirred and opened his eyes. As the chair was not in front of the altar, it was easy to miss. He stood up and stepped forward into Janet's view.

"Oh, I didn't see you there." Janet was surprised and shocked that another person was by her beloved altar. Jacob was just as surprised that someone else had found his secret site.

Neither one of them knew what to say to one another, but no one seemed eager to leave or even move. Jacob looked down at the young woman standing there. She was attractive, slim and well-dressed in a blazer and skirt; however, he noticed the runners that somehow didn't go with the outfit. Janet surveyed the older man and guessed him to be in his 70s, maybe early 80s. He had a good head of hair, which was quite grey, and he looked fit but she noticed that he had a cane. He wore a '70s-style tracksuit with clog-like shoes.

There was a rustle behind them, and a teenage boy approached on the path. He had his head down and was listening to his iPod, so he didn't immediately see the two other people near the altar. James looked up and was alarmed to see Janet and Jacob in his sacred spot. "Ah shit—busted!" James put his head down in dismay and was about to turn around and leave, when Jacob said, "Wait a minute, young man."

James came closer and saw the old dude and the business lady (with weird runners on), standing there looking like they had seen a ghost. Of course, they had seen the vision too. "Um, are you here because of the lady that appears here? James asked.

"What lady?" Janet stuck her chin out defiantly.

"Well, I thought, 'cause you are standing here where she comes and maybe you have seen her . . ." James was getting confused and a bit freaked out about what was going on.

Jacob sat heavily on the chair and spoke. "I think we all have seen the vision here, am I right?" James nodded and Janet reluctantly said, "Yes."

"So she has come to all of us. It was naive of me to think that she would only appear for me, and a little bit selfish. How long have you been coming here?" Jacob looked at both of them.

"I don't know for sure, but maybe a month," James said.

"About the same." Janet spoke softly.

"What does she look like?" Jacob asked.

"She's some kind of saint or something," James said.

"She's the Mother Mary." Janet spoke with more assurance and turned to Jacob. "What about you? Who is she to you?"

"She is the Mother Mary, I think, but I am Jewish , so what do I know? All I know is she is special and makes me feel . . . special." Jacob smiled.

"Yeah, she is fantastic, she makes me feel like everything is going to be okay, even when there is a lot of shit, oops, crap going on." James was getting excited as he spoke.

"She is the most beautiful thing I have ever seen and she makes me feel safe and well, so much more . . . I can't really put it into words." Janet's eyes shone with love as she spoke.

They were all silent for a while, not sure of what to say or do.

"I am not so sure she will come to all of us together like this," Jacob said aloud. "I have the feeling she won't ."

"Well, what do you suggest?" Janet said.

"Maybe we can take turns and come back on separate days and times, and see if she comes back." James was surprised at his own suggestion and that it made sense.

"Yes, I guess we could try that," Jacob said. "Maybe we could meet up next week and let each other know if she does come back." Jacob felt he needed to see these two people again.

Janet, on the other hand, wasn't that keen. "Not sure about that; I guess we could try it. I don't know that we have to meet up, though."

James didn't agree. "The old guy is right. We should meet up and let each of us know if she comes back."

"My name is Jacob." Jacob stood up and went over and shook hands with Janet and James.

"Mine is Janet."

"I'm James."

"Where should we meet up?" James ignored Janet's negativity and turned to Jacob.

"There is a Starbucks on Denman, across from Robson Street. How about we meet there?"

Janet relented. "Okay. When and what time?"

They discussed their schedules briefly and decided to meet the next Saturday at 11:00 a.m. Each one of them would come a different day and time next week to see if the vision came back to them.

They all parted at the same time and walked away silently.

Chapter 11

Janet

Janet was not happy about her encounter with the other two, James and Jacob. In fact, she was angry. She had just lost her job and gone to see her vision. Yes, her vision, and not one but two people had trespassed on her sacred place. To make matters worse, they had seen her as well.

Janet knew she was being irrational but she didn't care. She felt rejected again. All her life she had felt rejected—rejected by her biological mother, her adopted family, her career—and now this one special thing that she had was no longer hers alone; she had to share it with others. She vowed not to go there anymore and would be damned if she was going to meet up with the other two.

The anger stayed with her for two days and that transformed into hurt and then depression. Janet stayed in bed for two days when the depression hit. She couldn't eat and only had some water to drink. She cried and cried until her chest hurt and she felt exhausted by all the emotion. Janet missed her scheduled day and time. But she pretended that it didn't matter. She would no longer visit the site, she vowed.

Chapter 12

James

James reaction was the opposite of Janet's. He was relieved that someone else, well, two other people, had seen the same vision. He figured he was pretty special to be included in the appearance of the Mother Mary. He didn't really care if it was the Mother Mary or some other saint; he just knew she was special and awesome and made him feel better and not alone. It was great to have someone so powerful on his side.

James came home after that encounter and spoke to his mom about his sister and her condition. His mom didn't say much and James didn't really want to hear anything negative, so he kept the conversation short. He told his mom he was feeling better and even went to visit his sister that evening. She looked terrible and didn't have enough energy to speak much, but at least he saw her, and this made him and his parents feel better.

The specified day and time came and James went to the spot. He saw the altar and the stones and flowers. He waited for the vision to appear, but something didn't feel right. He had a sixth sense that she wasn't coming.

He stood there for over a half an hour, and still nothing happened. She wasn't coming. Had she finished her appearances? Did the three of them meeting up somehow jinx her showing again? Surprisingly, James didn't feel too bummed out about it. He still wanted to meet up with gramps and the other lady, to see if they'd had better luck.

Chapter 13

Jacob

Jacob felt slightly detached from the meeting. It was as if he were watching it from a distance and not actually in it. It seemed almost surreal. Did he really meet two other people that had seen the same vision? Did he actually set up a time and a place to meet up after their designated times and days to view the Mother Mary? Was he some kind of mediator in this?

Jacob's happiness faded temporarily. He became quiet and introverted for the rest of the week. Simone felt vindicated for suspecting that Jacob's good humour could not last. She did, however, refrain from saying anything. She also knew when to take a step back and see what would happen. Jacob did not even speak to Lorraine for a couple of evenings. Instead he went to bed early, too tired to even think about what he would say to Lorraine. He slept deeply and awoke feeling like he was drugged.

The day of his meeting with Mother Mary came, and he went to the sacred place, but he knew he would not see her. He waited for 10 minutes and then walked away, feeling more weary than he had in a long time. "What was going on?" he thought to himself. Even his usual bantering with himself seemed to stop and he just didn't think much about anything.

He was determined to go to Starbucks and see the other two. He had to see if they felt the same way.

Chapter 14

James and Jacob

James felt excited and nervous, like he was meeting a girl who was interested in him. He saw Jacob enter the coffee shop and called him over. Jacob sat down and asked what he wanted to drink. "I'll get it; tell me what you would like." James eagerly got up and waited until Jacob made his choice. Jacob smiled to himself and mistakenly thought James' exuberance was due to the fact that he had seen the vision. They sat in silence for awhile sipping their drinks, waiting for Janet to show. After 10 minutes had elapsed, Jacob said, "I don't think Jane is going to show."

"I think her name is Janet," James said.

"Oh, yes, Janet. Anyway, I don't think she is going to come. So, James, did you see our lovely lady?" Jacob asked, smiling.

"Well, no, I didn't actually. Did you?"

Jacob was surprised at this. "No, I didn't either . . ."

James pursed his lips. "Do you think she will come back?"

"I really don't know, but what bothers me is how different I feel after meeting the both of you."

"How do you feel different?"

"Well, before I met you both, I felt quite happy and light. Now I feel disjointed and heavy . . . not sure why . . . like I lost a part of myself . . . I just seemed to find myself; now it is lost again." Jacob smiled weakly.

"That's weird, because I feel totally stoked, like I am on a high, you know; I feel a part of something big and not sure what, but it feels good."

The two engaged in a discussion that went on for an hour. They talked a bit about their families, about Lorraine dying and Diana having this debilitating illness. They also talked about how the vision had changed things for them and what it meant to them. At the end of the hour, Jacob felt better and brighter than he had for the past week. James was practically glowing.

"I think we are not meant to see the vision on a particular day and time; it is something that shouldn't be planned. We should just go there, when we feel the need and see what happens."

James nodded in agreement. "Do you think it is okay if we meet up again?"

Jacob smiled. "I would like that very much. When do you want to meet?"

"Next Saturday, same time?" James asked.

"Sure, good idea . . . I wonder what happened to Janet."

Chapter 15

Janet

Janet felt like she had hit rock bottom. She felt very much alone and unwanted. The ridiculous thing was that the vision had made her feel safe and wanted, so why did it bother her so much that two other people had seen the same vision? Her expectations were totally outrageous and that in itself made her feel terrible. There was no way Janet was going to understand it, nor did she want to. She just wanted to leak out all this toxic mess that she had conjured up, real or not.

She went to her doctor to up her dosage of her anxiety medication. Her doctor could see Janet was going through something and suggested she go back to her therapist. Janet said she would think about it but, at the moment, just needed to be. With no job prospects, she started to claim employment benefits. The way she felt, it wasn't a good time to be looking for a job. Janet had not had any reason to cross the bridge, so she convinced herself that she wasn't in the area to visit the special site, anyway. Secretly, she wanted an excuse to go, but she couldn't think of anything.

She had received another letter from the ministry asking if she had made a decision to allow her biological mother to have contact with her. She was rereading the letter when the phone rang. She looked at the call display and saw that it was her parents calling. She wasn't going to answer it, but she hadn't spoken to them for nearly two weeks and felt guilty.

"Hello," Janet answered.

"Hello, dear. We haven't heard from you for a while and are wondering if everything is okay." Her mother did sound worried.

Janet had only superficial conversations with her parents. They didn't want to hear about her life and she didn't want to tell them anything about her life, so they just pretended that everything was okay and that they had a normal daughter and parent relationship. This time, Janet couldn't control her emotions.

"I, I . . . have not been well." Janet started to cry; she couldn't help it.

"Whatever is wrong? Do you want me to come out?"

"No, Mother, I have received letters from the ministry and my biological mother is asking to contact me."

"I see." Her mother suddenly went cold and distant.

"I guess you don't think it is a good idea, judging by your tone." Janet was equally cold and distant.

"Why would you ever want to see that woman? She has given you nothing, we have given you everything."

"Have you, Mother . . . given me everything?"

"Janet, what do you mean? Of course we have given you everything: a roof over your head, a brother, education . . ."

"I know I was a disappointment to you both; I know how you feel, Mother—I am not stupid."

"Janet, what has gotten into you? We are your parents; we love you."

"I am sorry, Mother, but I just don't buy it anymore. Look, it is not a good time to talk; I have to go." Before her mother could speak again, Janet hung up the phone.

Surprisingly, Janet felt quite liberated. She had finally spoken some of the truth that she had been suppressing all these years. Without hesitation, she grabbed her keys and got into her car. Bridge or no bridge, she knew where she had to go.

Chapter 16

James

It was weird. James was actually enjoying his meetings and conversations with Jacob. He couldn't wait for Saturday morning to come and shoot the breeze with the old guy. They just didn't talk about the vision, but about lots of stuff: school, his parents, his sister, sports and even what food they liked. What was even more surprising is that neither of them had gone back to see the vision. There wasn't any need. They knew she was there and for the moment that was all they needed. James had even been doing better in school. His grades were up and he hadn't skipped class. James had not smoked a joint for over a month—go figure.

The only downside was that his sister was not doing well. She was still in hospital and now she was being fed by a tube. James was trying to see her more often but it was hard. He hated the smell of the hospital, seeing all the other sick kids and, most of all, his sister just lying there, hardly responding. It didn't seem fair. What had she done to deserve that? What had anyone done to deserve their problems? Usually nothing, so it was sometimes hard to understand how the world worked. "It is what it is," as Todd B. would say. That was the other thing—James seemed to be thinking about so many random things. He never used to think that much. It seemed to him that he used to go around in a fog, just getting by. Now he looked where he was walking, and really appreciated details, and thought about what made the universe tick. Jacob had said that James was an old soul. James didn't quite get what he meant, but he liked the sound of it.

James was looking forward to their meeting tomorrow. He wondered what had happened to Janet.

Chapter 17

Jacob

Jacob was busier now than he had been before he retired. Sure, he worked, but that was about all he did. He used to come home and have supper with Lorraine, watch TV and then go to bed and start all over again the next day. "Sheesh, what an existence." Jacob reprimanded himself. "Oh, well, I didn't know any better."

Jacob was trying to be kinder to himself and, like the vision, forgive himself for all his wrongdoings in the past. "If Mary can find it in her heart, then so should I," he thought. Now, Jacob went to the seniors' centre three days a week, started helping in the food bank once a week and still did his daily walking; and of course there were Saturday mornings with James. If he had had a grandson, he would have wished him to be like James. What a great kid. James was genuinely interested in what Jacob had to say. They talked about anything and everything. It was fun to be with someone so much younger and just beginning his life. It was strange but neither of them had been back to see the vision. They talked about her and what a difference it had made in their lives, but there seemed no urgency, like before, to be in her presence.

"I am sure it will happen when it is meant to," Jacob reflected. "Humph, I am beginning to sound like a wise old man." Jacob chuckled to himself as he made his way to the coffee shop.

Chapter 18

Janet

Janet had returned to the clearing and was standing before the altar. "If there is ever a time I need to see you, now is the time, Mother Mary." Closing her eyes, Janet knelt before the altar and felt the familiar breeze. She looked up and saw the beautiful vision of the Mother Mary. As before, she was illuminated; however, the smile was gone and there were tears running down her face. Janet gasped as she saw this. "Oh, please don't cry, don't cry for me. I was foolish and selfish and I am here now; I know you love me and will always be with me."

Janet was crying herself. She felt so much love for this woman standing before her that her heart seemed to ache with the strength of it. The smile on Mary returned once more and she held her hands out to Janet in understanding. "Thank you, thank you for being here, for being with me. I am so grateful." Janet was smiling through her tears. The vision gradually faded and Janet was alone once more. "How could I have been so stupid?" she asked herself.

Janet got up from the ground and dusted herself off. She didn't wear the runners that were under the bush, even though they were still there. She had her own running shoes on. For some reason she found this funny and started to laugh. She was still laughing as she came from out of the path. It felt good to laugh again. She hadn't done that for such a long time. She looked at her watch and it was nearly 11:00 a.m. She suddenly felt very thirsty and hungry. Then it struck Janet. The meeting place that Jacob and—oh, she couldn't remember the teenager's name—John or something would go to on a Saturday. She wondered if they still went there. There was only one way to find out. Janet jogged along Georgia to Denman and up to Starbucks.

Chapter 19

Janet, Jacob and James

For a Saturday morning, Starbucks was not that busy. There were quite a few tables available. James had arrived first and sat down in their usual spot. He was texting on his phone when Jacob walked in. "I believe it is my turn for drinks." Jacob waved away James' attempt to get to the counter. As Jacob was ordering, Janet came in, slightly winded from her jog up. Neither James or Jacob recognized her.

She had her hair pulled back in a ponytail and no makeup. She was also dressed in capri pants and a t-shirt. She didn't look like the businesswoman that they'd originally met. Janet saw James straight away and sat down opposite him. "Remember me?" Janet asked tentatively. James looked at her for a minute and then smiled. "Janet, right?"

Janet sighed with relief. "Yeah, I . . . look, I'm sorry I didn't come before . . ." Jacob came up to them and studied Janet for a minute. "Jane, is that right?" he questioned.

"Janet, and you are Jacob and . . ." She looked towards James, who responded, "James, my name is James." They all smiled at one another.

Jacob put down the drinks he was holding and said to Janet, "What can I get you?"

Janet got up in protest but Jacob shooed her down again. "Let me be a gentleman and buy you a coffee." Janet laughed and told Jacob what she wanted. James and Janet stayed silent until Jacob sat down again with Janet's coffee.

"For starters, I want to apologise for not meeting with you that first time. I . . . well, I had a lot going on and, oh what the hell, I might as well admit, I was jealous." Janet actually blushed at her confession. Jacob smiled but didn't say anything and James looked confused.

"I don't know, I just felt like someone had taken something away from me, like it wasn't mine anymore, or it didn't belong to me . . . Stupid, I know, but I . . . that's how I felt. It brought up some other stuff that I won't go into and I was quite depressed for a while, well, actually until today, and I had a fight with my mother over the phone and I had to come and see . . ."—Janet lowered her voice—"the vision."

"You saw her today?" James asked, excited.

"Yes, not too long ago." Janet smiled at the memory of her.

"You see, Janet, we have not seen her for a long time," Jacob interjected.

"You haven't seen her since we last met? What about your scheduled times?"

"She didn't show. I guess she does not work on mortal time." Jacob laughed at this.

"But we have been meeting here ever since, just talking and stuff . . ." James seemed at bit embarrassed by this admission.

"Wow, that's great. I mean, not that you didn't see her but that you meet up every week."

Jacob said, "It has been very gratifying. James and I have found a lot of common interests, which is amazing considering I am an old crock, and we enjoy our chats together."

James laughed. "You are not an old crock. He has taught me some really cool stuff."

Janet looked at both of them and could see the admiration they had for each other in their eyes. Normally Janet would have assumed that she was not needed or wanted but she felt a connection with the two of them and wanted to join them.

"Is it okay if I chat with you as well?" she asked.

"Sure, of course," they both said together.

"Tell us what has been going on in your life," Jacob said.

Janet began to unfold her story and they sat for two hours talking, laughing and enjoying each other's company.

Chapter 20

James

The trio had met up for three Saturdays now and it was like they had always been together, meeting and discussing anything and everything. At first James thought Janet was a loser, and he didn't mean that in an unkind way, but, hey, being so afraid of everything, that was weird.

James thought about it a lot and then began to feel sorry for her. Being given away by your own mom, not really cared for by her adopted parents and then being scared of her own shadow. That was tough. It made James put himself in someone else's place instead of thinking about his own sorry life. After thinking about it all and processing it, he actually liked Janet. She was nice looking and kind. And he could tell she liked him and Jacob.

After Janet's last visit with the vision, none of them had been back. They were all pretty chilled at present and felt good. Not that everything was great, but they felt that they could handle their lives at the moment.

James' sister was still in hospital and there was no change really. He barely saw his parents but his dad had moved back in, which he thought was great. His dad was sleeping in the spare bedroom, but it was better than him living in that crummy apartment he rented. The next big event coming up for James was a year-end dance. He wasn't all that bothered about it, but all his friends were going and they were bringing dates. James kept telling himself he didn't want to go, but really he did and there was a girl he was interested in, Lisa. She was a year younger and pretty, and he could tell she liked him. He just had to man-up and ask her. James was thinking about going to see Mother Mary and ask for help with it, but that seemed a bit of a lame reason to ask for guidance. Anyway, the dance was not for a while and he would have plenty of time to ask Lisa. Maybe he would discuss it with his friends, and James smiled as he thought of "his friends." James would never in a million years have thought he would call Janet and Jacob his friends, but that is what they were—very good friends.

Chapter 21

Jacob

Jacob dozed in his chair after lunch. He had meant to go to the food bank to help out, but he felt too tired. He wasn't sure what was going on, but he didn't have his usual energy. His daily walks had become an effort. He seemed to have to rest more often than not. "Maybe I am coming down with the flu or something," Jacob mused. "What the heck, I never get sick."

And it was true—Jacob rarely got any kind of virus, not even the sniffles. "I am spending more time around people; maybe I have to build up my immune system or something. Simone is always going on about the immune system. I'm not even sure what it is." Jacob picked up Lorraine's picture. "What do you think Lorraine, what is ailing me?" Just last week, Simone had said that Jacob was looking pale and maybe he should go to the doctor. Jacob hated the doctors, especially after all the time they had spent with the doctors when Lorraine got sick.

"I'm fine. Look, I am an old man; no wonder I am tired," Jacob protested to Simone. She laughed but he could see she was not convinced.

Jacob didn't like the look Lorraine was giving him (or what he perceived that she was giving him) and he sighed deeply. "Okay, sweetheart, if I don't feel better by next week, I will make an appointment with the doctor. Satisfied?" And with that, Jacob put down the picture and fell asleep.

Chapter 22

Janet

Janet had paid for a year's subscription to the yoga studio, so she was still able to go. She was so grateful for her insight about doing this. She really needed it right now, especially being out of work and on the road to what she liked to call her "wellness." Janet loved the gentler yoga classes, such as hatha and yin. She would practise her breathing and feel a calmness come over her. Whenever she did Savasana—the total relaxation position—Janet would always picture Mother Mary and the beautiful light that surrounded her.

Another practice of Janet's was her "gratitudes." One of yoga teachers mentioned that being grateful raises your vibrational frequency and puts you in a better space. From then on, Janet listed 10 "gratitudes" per day and these always made her feel better. One of the main ones was her newfound friendship with James and Jacob. She could not have asked for better friends and she was delighted that they felt the same way. "What a strange world this is," Janet said to herself as she thought about encountering the vision, meeting James and Jacob and pretty much starting over.

Since her last phone call with her mother, Janet tried hard to be less judgemental with her family. She knew that they really did believe they had given her everything, and they had not shortchanged her in material ways, just emotional. Janet had decided to write a letter to her parents and explain how she felt. She had two drafts but she didn't like either of them. She left it for now because she just couldn't find the right words.

Janet had called the ministry about meeting with her biological mother and asked if they could give her more time. It was not to say that she wouldn't meet up with her but that she had to think about it some more. The woman at the ministry was very nice and told Janet that if she wanted, they would put her in touch with a counsellor that specializes in these issues (free of charge). Janet took the name and telephone number from the woman and said she would be in touch when she had reached a decision. Janet tucked the number of the counsellor away in her drawer; she wasn't ready to go there yet.

Janet looked at the want ads for a job and there was nothing she had enough experience or the training for. Finding a job this time around was not going to be easy, she knew that, and she was toying with the idea of doing something different, something totally out of her comfort zone. She looked at the college courses and then the BCIT courses for vocational training. After meeting and being with Jacob, she wondered what it would be like to work as a care-aide in a nursing home or as a companion to the elderly. If she went to school, it would be different this time around. She was better equipped to handle her panic attacks and the classes would be smaller and she would be doing something she liked. Janet was beginning to get excited about her prospects. She truly felt that this was a possibility. She could hardly wait to discuss it with James and Jacob.

Chapter 23

Janet, James and Jacob

Whenever the three met up at Starbucks, they always got their same table. "It is definitely meant to be," Janet said. She could barely contain her excitement and was all but springing out of her chair. Jacob smiled and leaned over to her. "What has gotten you so riled up? You have ants in your pants." Janet laughed. "Well, I think I am going to sign up for a course at one of the colleges. I would learn how to be a "health care support worker," and this would mean I could work in hospitals or nursing homes or be a visiting companion."

"What, like Simone?" Jacob asked.

"Yes, I guess so. It is a three-year course, but I would get a better job and with the escalating elderly population, there is a lot of scope for it." Janet could not stop smiling.

"You mean there are a lot old grumps like me around?" Jacob pointed to his chest.

"Well, yes, but you are not an old grump." Janet gently touched Jacob's hand.

Jacob smiled and said, "I think it is a wonderful idea, but how will you afford it?"

"I did get a severance pay from my last job and I am good at saving up, so I will be fine. I will probably have to get some kind of cleaning job or waitressing job on the weekends as well, but that's okay."

"What about your panic issues?" James spoke at last.

"Yeah, well, I will have to work at it but I am determined. I need to do this." Janet spoke with conviction.

Jacob noticed how quiet James was. He was normally full of beans, but not today.

"What is up with you, young man?" Jacob looked intently at James.

"Oh, nothing, I . . . well, I want to ask this girl out, to the year-end dance and I am kind of, well, don't know how to ask her, you know . . ." James was getting redder and redder.

"Ah, you want advice from us?" Jacob pointed to Janet and himself. Janet looked down at the table, swirling her cup around. "You won't get any advice from me; I have no idea." Janet spoke honestly.

Jacob puffed up his chest like a prize rooster. "Well, James, I may be old but I do know a thing or two about charming women. You should see me at the seniors' centre. The old dears are cooing all over me. Not that I am interested—there was only one woman for me . . ."

James couldn't help but smile—taking advice from an 80-year-old, that was really cool.

"Don't be too coy or she will think you are not interested, but don't be too pushy either. Maybe ask her if she wants to go out for a soda"—James rolled his eyes upward— "or whatever it is you do nowadays. But don't ask her straight after that. Leave it for a couple of days and then ask her out again. After about the third time, you ask her if she is interested in going to the dance. See what she says. If she says yes, then say, 'Well, what about going with me?'"

"If she says no, just play it cool and don't let her know she has hurt your feelings. There are plenty more fish in the sea."

"You may have something there, Gramps." James had given Jacob that nickname.

"Have you got a boyfriend, Janet?" James knew the answer, but he wanted to hear what she said about it.

"Ah, sadly, no, I have had only one boyfriend and he turned out to be a bit of a jerk. I was thinking about joining one of the online dating services, but I think I want to sort some stuff out first before I dive in there." Janet smiled weakly.

Jacob nodded. "Very wise decision, my dear, and I am not so sure about those online dating thingamajiggies. You should be careful who you meet up with. There can be some nasty predators out there."

"I know, Jacob, but it is so hard to meet guys now. It can be very intimidating and it is nice to know if you have something in common."

"What do you think they would say about the vision? Would you mention it?" James asked.

"Well, not straight away, but it is important to me, so yes I would. What about you with this girl?

"Nah, it's only a dance, I am not going to marry the chick or anything." James dismissed the idea.

"James, you are funny." Janet couldn't help but laugh.

Jacob was noticeably quieter and he seemed to shrink into himself. There was a look of pain on his face.

"What's wrong, Jacob?" Janet asked, concerned.

"I just got a pain, a bit of indigestion, maybe. Sometimes coffee doesn't agree with me." Jacob winced a bit.

"Hey, Gramps, you don't look so good. Do you want to go home?"

"Yes, I think I will . . . I don't like to ask, but can you give me a lift, Janet?"

"Of course, come on." She held onto Jacob's arm and helped him out of the coffee shop and into her car.

"See you next week, James, and good luck with the girl." Jacob called out to James as he hopped onto his bike. "Yeah, see ya next week, hope you feel better," James called back.

Janet didn't say much to Jacob apart from asking where he lived. They arrived at his house and Janet helped him to the door. "I will be all right now, my dear, thank you so much." Jacob didn't like to be fussed over.

"Do you want me to call someone? Simone?" Janet asked.

"No, no, I will be fine . . . There is one thing," Jacob started

"Yes?"

"I have made an appointment to go to my doctor next Tuesday. Would you mind going with me? I know that sounds pathetic but—"

"Stop it, Jacob, of course I will go with you. What time?"

"It's at 2:00 p.m. If you come here at one, we will have plenty of time to get there."

"Okay, and are you sure you don't want me to stay?"

"No, I am going to have a lay down and I will be fine. This will be a good test for you to see if you really do want to work with oldies like me." Jacob smiled through his pain.

"Yes, it will be. Are you sure you are okay?"

"Yes, now go."

"Okay, see you next Tuesday at one. Bye, Jacob." Janet closed the door behind her. She did not have a good feeling about this.

Chapter 24

Jacob

Jacob and Janet sat in the doctor's office. The doctor smiled pleasantly. "What can I do for you, Jacob?" he asked.

Jacob found it difficult to speak. His mouth and tongue felt extremely dry like he hadn't had a drink in a while. The doctor looked a bit perplexed. Janet spoke up.

"Jacob hasn't been feeling well, lately. He has been very fatigued and recently has been having pain in his abdomen." Jacob smiled gratefully.

"And you are?" the doctor asked.

"She is a good friend, looking out for me." Jacob patted Janet's hand.

The doctor set about listening to Jacob's chest, taking his blood pressure and pulse and feeling his abdomen. Jacob winced a few times when the doctor pressed on certain areas. The doctor pulled down the bottom of Jacob's eyelid. "You look a bit anemic," he said. "I am going to get some blood work done. Have your bowel movements changed? Are you urinating more? Is it painful?"

Jacob looked uncomfortable. "Well, at my age, what is normal? I go but it is not always regular and I have to get up twice a night to pee, ahem, urinate, but it is not painful."

"Have you ever had a colonoscopy?" the doctor asked.

"No, I have not," Jacob said.

"Well, I am going to schedule you for a colonoscopy and a scope at the same time. You seem to be in good health otherwise—strong heart, good lungs—but I want to check out the colon and the abdomen, et cetera. It is a safe procedure and can tell us a lot. Anything else I can do for you?"

Jacob knew they were being dismissed.

Janet spoke up. "How long will it be before he has the procedure?"

"I am going to see if I can speed it up, so it won't be long. My receptionist will give you the necessary requisition for the lab work and the directions of what you need to do before the colonoscopy. We will contact you when we have a date and time for the procedure." The doctor stood up and shook Jacob's and Janet's hands.

They received the necessary paperwork and walked out of the medical centre.

Janet suggested they go for a coffee somewhere and Jacob nodded gratefully. He was feeling overwhelmed by it all. He had expected to just be given some prescription and everything would be fine, but to have some kind of hospital procedure didn't sit well with him.

They sat by a table away from everyone, in comfortable overstuffed chairs that were becoming the norm in coffee houses. Jacob didn't say anything for a while and Janet wisely let him be in his own thoughts. They drank in a comfortable silence. Finally, Jacob spoke.

"Sorry about all the bathroom talk. I didn't expect the doctor to ask such personal questions."

Janet just smiled and let Jacob carry on.

"When Lorraine and I were trying to have children, it was so difficult for her. She had every kind of test imaginable and she told me that she lost all of her intimate privacy to the doctors and specialists, like she was some kind of lab rat. Then when she got breast cancer, she had both her breasts removed, lost her hair to chemotherapy and felt physically violated again.

You know she wouldn't undress in front of me after that. I told her I loved her no matter what, but she wouldn't listen. She could have had reconstructive surgery, but then they found the cancer had moved to her liver, so it was too late . . ." Silent tears rolled down Jacob's face and Janet held his hand. She felt privileged to be listening to Jacob's deep-buried agonies.

"I have a feeling that I will start to understand how she felt . . . I don't mind telling you, Janet, that I am scared."

"I will be with you, Jacob, I will be with you all the way." Janet whispered. Jacob knew she was speaking from the heart.

Chapter 25

James

James wasn't sure what was going on. Janet and Jacob seemed pretty tight-lipped about Jacob's health concerns. At the last Saturday get-together, they said that Jacob had to have some procedure and that he was anemic. He knew they were holding something back but didn't push it. Part of him didn't want to go there, especially as his sister was going through her own medical nightmare. His parents seemed to be getting on better, but they were hardly home.

James felt like a roommate rather than a son. He had to fend more and more for himself. He was getting tired of cooking Kraft Dinner and wieners for supper. What he wouldn't give for a nice wholesome dinner. His friends thought it was great that James could basically be left to his own devices. James didn't look at it that way. In some way, he felt he was being tested, not by his parents but by himself. He stayed at home at night and did his homework. He kept the place clean and even did his own laundry. "What a loser," he joked to himself, but he carried on being responsible.

He even asked Lisa out for an ice cream at the local DQ. It went okay. She didn't say much; he mainly talked about school and stuff. James didn't mention his sister or his friends, Janet and Jacob. It went okay as far as he was concerned and he would take Jacob's advice and ask her out again, but not for a while. Had to play it cool. "Taking advice from an old guy, what a trip." James laughed at himself. He suddenly felt a pang of anguish in his heart, thinking about Jacob and what was going on. James quickly dismissed it and got back to the dishes.

Chapter 26

Janet

Janet was as good as her word about being with Jacob. He had the blood work done and found that he was very anemic, which accounted for his fatigue and some of his discomfort. He was put on iron supplements, and Simone was cooking iron-enriched foods. He was also drinking prune juice to counter the effect of the constipating iron tablets. Jacob protested loudly about the change in medication and diet. "Why do I have to eat all this spinach and beans and the God-awful prune juice?" Jacob made a face.

Janet laughed. "Jacob, you have to get more iron in you and the prune juice helps you go to the bathroom. Besides, you are having a steak once a week, which you love, so enjoy that." They would have their friendly banter and Janet would come over twice a week and play Scrabble or just talk. She went for a walk with him along the seawall but Jacob's energy was greatly diminished. One evening when she sat with him, watching TV, she asked him, "Jacob, why don't you go and see the Mother Mary and, you know, have a chat with her about your situation."

"I had thought about it, Janet, but we don't even know what is going on yet, apart from being anemic, and I don't know, I don't feel it is right..."

"What do you mean?"

"Asking for myself, asking for some healing for myself. I guess I am old school. I come from a time when you take it on the chin and you don't ask for help with these things. Besides, what will be will be, as Doris Day would say." Jacob gave Janet a weak smile.

Janet decided she would take matters into her own hands. The next day, she went to the spot in the park where the running shoes were, and even though she was wearing sensible shoes, she put on the familiar pair. She approached the path and walked up to the altar. Everything was the same as always. She knelt down in front of the altar and closed her eyes. "Please, Mother Mary, can you help our friend Jacob? He is not well, and I am afraid it is something serious. Can you help heal him?"

Janet felt the gentle breeze and the warmth of the light shining on her. She opened her eyes and looked up at the beautiful apparition before her. Mother Mary held her hands out to Janet and she could see her smiling, but it was a sad smile. The pain of the realization struck Janet in her heart and she gasped aloud. "Oh, Mary, why can't it be different? I have just found him, and now this..."

Janet acknowledged the selfishness of her statement. "I am sorry, Mary. I don't want Jacob to suffer; I want him to be happy and healthy." Janet could feel the shift in the vision's being and then saw Mary's usual smile. Janet was confused as to whether Mother Mary meant that Jacob would be healed or whether she meant something else. The vision vanished and Janet could feel the ground beneath her knees.

Janet felt better but not completely sure of what was going to happen. She felt her phone vibrate in her pocket. She answered it. "Hello."

"Janet, it's Jacob; I got the call just a few moments ago. I am going in for the colonoscopy next Monday. Would you mind coming over and help me get the concoctions that I need to buy before the procedure?"

Janet could feel the anxiety in his voice. "Of course, Jacob, I will be there right away." She replaced the runners with her own shoes and went to Jacob's.

Chapter 27

Jacob

The following week went by in a bit of a whirlwind. Janet helped Jacob get ready for the colonoscopy and took him to the hospital to have it done. About two days later, Jacob got a phone call from the doctor to come and see him as soon as possible, and it would be a good idea if he brought his friend. Jacob knew straight away it was not good news even before the phone call. He'd had a dream the night after the procedure. Lorraine and the Mother Mary were in it. He could see them in the distance, their heads together, bending over and whispering to one another. He shouted out to them and then they turned to him but walked away. Jacob felt very sad but then he could feel someone beside him, and he looked to see Janet standing next to him, holding his hand. He woke up then and knew.

Janet and Jacob sat in exactly the same places they had before and listened to the diagnosis that they both expected to hear.

"I'm afraid it is cancer. It is located in your colon, for the most part, and we need to operate as soon as possible to remove it. We are not sure, but you may need a catheter for your bowels after the op, which may be temporary—or not. You will then have to have a series of chemo treatments." Jacob stopped listening after the doctor said cancer. Even though he knew it was cancer, he didn't like it being confirmed. He always thought he would be taken by a heart attack, like his father, and his father before him. He didn't know of anyone in his blood family that had ever had cancer. And the colon, maybe it was because he had been a shit his whole life. Jacob snickered at the pun, and Janet and the doctor looked oddly at him.

"I'm sorry, I was thinking of something else. I am glad you are here, Janet, because I have missed most of what the doctor has been saying." Jacob spoke with honesty.

"That is normal, which is why we ask for someone to come with you." He smiled kindly.

Janet asked, "When will the surgery take place?"

"It will probably be in the next week or so. It is best to get as much rest in the meantime and eat and drink healthily, which I understand you have been doing. We will contact you as soon as we have a space available for surgery." The doctor stood up which was their cue to leave. Janet thanked the doctor, and Jacob shook his hand weakly.

Neither of them spoke but they went directly to the same coffee shop that they'd stopped at previously. They ordered their drinks and sat down. Janet took a sip of her coffee and said matter-of-factly, "Do you think Simone will be okay to cook for me when I move in to look after you?"

Jacob didn't skip a beat. "You can use me as your reference when you register for your care-aide course. You will have first-hand experience."

"That's what I was counting on." She squeezed Jacob's hand. They finished their drinks silently, deep in their own thoughts.

Chapter 28

James

"This is crazy, man, you can't be sick, I don't believe it." James was angry. He didn't want to be reasonable—he just wanted to vent. "First my sister, now you; this is unbelievable." James was almost shouting. Janet put a hand on his arm to soothe him, which he promptly shook off.

"James, you have to calm down, or else we will have to leave." Jacob motioned to the other patrons at the Starbucks. James sat down finally but his energy was still frazzing.

"James, it is fine; I will have the operation and the treatment and it will be fine." Jacob gave James a tentative smile, but James wasn't buying any of it.

"How goes it with your girlfriend?" Jacob tried to change the subject.

"She is not my girlfriend." James clearly did not want to talk about anything.

"Look, I gotta get out of here, I will see you later." James jumped up and ran out of the coffee shop.

James started riding his bike as fast as he could, weaving in and out of traffic. If he wanted to get himself involved in an accident, he was doing a pretty good job of trying.

He eventually made his way to the park and rode his bike into the sacred path. He threw his bike down and started to cry. "It is not fair, it's not fucking fair." James sat on the hard ground, throwing dirt at the altar. The light came quickly and hurt his tear-filled eyes. He had to wipe them several times before he could focus. There she was, holding her hands out to him in sympathy and kindness. "Why," he asked, "why? . . ." Mary continued to hold out her hands and gradually James felt her calming presence becoming ingrained into his being. He felt a healing and an acceptance. His tears had stopped and the inner turmoil was peaceful now. The light faded and James got up. He picked up his bike and rode back home.

Chapter 29

Janet

Janet felt she was in a coping mode. She didn't have time to think about anything except looking after Jacob and doing whatever was necessary for him. She moved into his spare bedroom the very next day after the doctor's diagnosis. Simone welcomed Janet's presence and was grateful for her ability to take charge of the situation, and do whatever was necessary to take care of Jacob.

Janet and Simone got on like a house on fire. They laughed and joked about anything and everything. Janet liked Simone's sense of humour and her ability to make light of serious situations. Simone was truly a shining light for both Janet and Jacob. Janet learned how to cook healthy and tasty meals from Simone. She also learned how to deal with Jacob's moodiness. Simone didn't take any crap from Jacob. She scolded, cajoled and fought with him. Janet sometimes watched open-mouthed at the way the two of them spoke to one another. They would often have an argument and not speak to one another for the rest of Simone's shift and then, the next day, treat each other as if nothing had been said the day before.

"I am French Canadian; you have to understand our culture," she would say to Janet. "We are very passionate about everything, but then the emotion disappears after a while. I can't stay mad at Jacob, he is too important to me."

Janet just shook her head and let them get on with it. Janet had more important things to concentrate on: Jacob was scheduled to go into surgery next week.

Chapter 30

Jacob

Jacob could see Lorraine, Janet and Simone standing together and laughing. He wondered what they were laughing at. He moved closer to them and they started pointing and covering their faces, trying to conceal their mirth. Jacob didn't understand why they were laughing. He looked down at himself and realized he didn't have any pants or underwear on. All of his private areas were missing. Jacob tried to shout at them to stop laughing but nothing was coming out. He seemed to be coming to the surface of a dream, but it was difficult to wake up. He felt heavy and his throat was extremely dry. He could hear someone in the background. "Jacob, can you hear me? You are in the recovery room, after your operation."

Jacob opened his eyes and could see a nurse with a surgical mask on, standing over him.

"There you are. You were an excellent patient and the operation went well." He could see her eyes crinkle up in a smile.

Jacob felt like a ton weight—he didn't seem to be able to move very well, and his throat was so dry.

"Can I have some water?" he croaked out.

"In a little while, my dear, we just have to let you come around. I know your throat is sore from the tube we have to insert. Try to swallow a few times."

Jacob did as he was told and it felt a bit better. He closed his eyes again, and the next thing he knew, he was in a hospital room. Even though he was sharing a room, he was lucky to have his bed near the window. It was a beautiful sunny day.

Janet suddenly appeared at his bedside. She held his hand. "Jacob, how are you feeling?" she asked, concerned.

"Like someone hit me with a hammer." Jacob smiled weakly as he said it.

Janet laughed. "Well, the doctor said the operation went extremely well, and they got all the cancer. They didn't even have to insert a catheter, which is good news."

"That is wonderful. Janet, can I have some water? . . ." Jacob sipped some water from a cup and sank back down on his pillows. "Water never tasted so good."

"I have to leave you now to rest, but I will be back later." Janet bent down to kiss his forehead. Jacob closed his eyes and promptly fell asleep.

All Jacob kept hearing from the nurses was what a good patient he was. He didn't think he was doing anything exceptional, but he was doing as he was told and not complaining, so I guess that is why he was a good patient. He felt very little discomfort and he was on a low dose of pain killers. Jacob still couldn't believe he had cancer, had the operation and was now cancer-free. It was still hard for him to comprehend all that had happened. He just wanted to go home and get back to his routine. The food was awful as far as he was concerned. He was spoiled by Simone's and now Janet's cooking. Simone had come in to visit the day after the operation and brought in some homemade bran muffins. "They will help you get back to normal." She winked at him. "I am doing some spring cleaning while you are in here. The place is looking spick and span," Simone was happy to report to Jacob.

"Don't kill yourself, Simone; you always keep the place like a palace."

Simone blushed with gratitude at Jacob's statement.

Jacob even had a few visits from some of the members of the seniors' centre. He was over the moon that they would find him worthy enough to visit. By the end of the week, he was up and walking to the sunroom on his own. He looked out at the trees nearby and the beautiful planted garden just below him. "I will not take any of this for granted again," Jacob vowed.

Someone came up behind him, while he was looking at the view.

"Hi, Gramps!"

"James." Jacob turned around and saw James standing there with a box of Purdy's chocolates in his hands.

"How are you doing?" James asked

"Good, good, I feel pretty good and will hopefully be out in a few days."

Jacob could see James was feeling awkward. "Sit here, next to me, and look at this view." He motioned James to sit on a seat facing the window.

"What are you looking at?" James asked, not seeming to understand what was so great about the view.

"The trees and the flowers and, well, everything is so much brighter and clearer and just wonderful." Jacob sighed.

"Did you have an eye operation as well?" James asked confused.

"No, no, it's just that after getting such bad news about having cancer and then the operation, it makes you appreciate everything so much more."

"Oh."

"I am glad you came, James. Janet and I were worried about you," Jacob said, still looking out the window.

"Yeah, I'm sorry I ran out on you that time. I just kind of lost it." James hung his head sheepishly. "I went and saw the vision and she, well, she made me feel better . . ."

"I am glad, James. The vision seems to be there when we need her the most."

"Yeah, it is nice to have someone to lean on." James smiled.

"What has been going on in your life?" Jacob asked

"The same old. My sister is the same but I did ask Lisa out a few times. I haven't asked her to the dance yet, but I will. I think she likes me." James blushed with this statement.

"What's not to like? You are a fine young man; she will be very happy to go to the dance with you, I know it," Jacob proclaimed.

"Thanks for the advice, Gramps, and thanks for, well, thanks for being there for me."

Jacob had to stop the tears from welling up in his eyes. He knew it would embarrass James if he started crying. "Ah, um, can you walk me back, James? I think I need to rest now."

"Sure."

They walked back to Jacob's room in silence, each grateful for the other's company.

Jacob went home after two more days in hospital. He got a list of the days and times he had to report to chemotherapy. It wasn't going to be a long process, once a week for six weeks and a very low dose. Jacob was glad that Janet was there to go over the details with the nurse.

"You may feel some discomfort after the chemo, but generally it disappears after the first few days. Don't be alarmed about the loss of appetite as well. That will disappear shortly after. Best thing you can do is just go with whatever you feel. Rest, eat light and don't expect too much." The nurse was explaining the symptoms to Jacob and Janet. Jacob was not paying too much attention—he felt it a bit overwhelmed and Janet was there to get all the information.

When they got home, a waft of homemade cooking entered Jacob's nostrils. "Ah, that smells delicious. Is it my favourite?" Jacob was licking his lips already.

"It sure is, Simone made it especially for you. Come in and sit down." Janet ushered Jacob into the living room. He sat in his well-worn chair and looked around at the newly polished furniture and shining windows. He gave a grateful sigh of relief and turned on the TV.

"It is so good to be home!"

The following week, Jacob started the chemotherapy treatment at the cancer clinic. It was a very unassuming place with a few beds and mostly chairs. There were magazines and a volunteer tea lady who would give you coffee, tea and cookies if you wanted. The nurses were all kind and informative. Jacob got hooked up to his IV and, after a couple of hours, he was finished. Janet stayed with him the whole time. She read for a bit as

Jacob dozed through most of the treatment. They gave him some Gravol to counteract the sickness that is sometimes felt with the chemo, and this made him sleepy. When they got home, Jacob lay down. After about an hour, he awoke to a very nauseated feeling in his stomach. He had to quickly dash to the bathroom to be sick. He felt like hell the rest of the day but refused any further anti-nauseating drugs from Janet. He hated how dopey he felt on them. Jacob only managed some Jell-O and yoghurt for the rest of the day. The effects of the chemo lasted two days, and by the third day, he was feeling better—not 100 percent, but better. He didn't remember Lorraine going through any of this, or had he conveniently forgotten?

The following week was much the same and he looked forward to the third day after the chemo, as he would start to feel better. On the third week of his treatment, he sat next to an attractive middle-aged woman. She had a scarf over her head, so Jacob assumed she had lost her hair, like Lorraine had. Jacob's hair was thinning slightly but it wasn't a huge issue for him. He did feel sorry for women going through chemo and losing their hair, as it must make them very self-conscious. It had for Lorraine. Janet was not able to sit with him that day, as she had to run some errands, but she promised to be back to take him home.

The lady smiled at Jacob and said, "I would shake hands but they are tied up at the moment."

Jacob smiled. "Hello, my name is Jacob."

"I'm Patty. You haven't been here very long," Patty observed.

"No, this is my third week, and I only have to come for three more weeks, I hope." Jacob crossed his free hand.

"Lucky you, I am a veteran here. This is my second year of treatment. I had quite aggressive breast cancer and had one round of treatment for six months and then I went into remission, but it came back, so I am back at it again." Patty had a resigned look on her face.

"I am sorry; my wife had breast cancer. She, um, died . . . two years ago." Jacob felt bad saying that his wife had passed away, but he couldn't lie.

"It sucks, doesn't it? Cancer, I mean . . . and the treatment, and there are no guarantees. What kind of cancer do you have?" Patty asked.

"Uh, colon cancer, but they said they got it all after the operation."

"Yeah, they say that, but you don't know where the buggers will show up next; they hide, ya see, and then reappear later." Patty could see Jacob's horrified face.

"Oh, I am sorry; I have a big mouth, and I am only speaking from my experience, so just ignore me."

"Oh, I understand. When my wife had it, we thought it was gone and then it appeared in her liver." Jacob shrugged his shoulders.

"Do you believe in God, Jacob?" Patty asked like she was asking for a napkin or something.

"Well, as a matter of fact, I do." Jacob thought for a minute and smiled. "And other things . . ."

"Yeah, I never really believed in anything until I got cancer and now I have had time to think long and hard about what it all means to be here . . . on this earth, I mean, and why things happen. It certainly makes it easier to believe in something up there"—Patty motioned her head towards the ceiling—"when you are going through a life-and-death situation."

They sat in silence for a bit.

"Hey, what do you think about the "Smart Meters" they are putting in? I think the government should give us a choice about it . . ."

Jacob and Patty spent the rest of the afternoon talking about subjects that are normally off-limits—religion and politics. "I guess cancer gives you free reign to talk about anything," Jacob would muse later.

After Jacob's last chemo treatment, he was more than happy to put it behind him. He had a healthy red blood count and been given the all-clear by his doctor. He didn't have to see the doctor again (unless there were problems) for another three months. When the effects of the last chemo had sufficiently worn off, Jacob took Janet, Simone and James out for dinner to the Keg.

"Order whatever you want. I just want to thank all of you for helping me with my recovery." Jacob held up his glass of water. "Here's to good health and happiness."

"Here, here, cheers!" After everyone clinked glasses together, they settled down to looking at the menu.

"Oh, my goodness, look at the prices." Simone was "tsking."

"I thought I was Jewish, not you," Jacob teased her. "Anyway, I am paying, so no looking at how much it costs."

They all had a wonderful time, with the good food and their companionship. When the three of them were busy chatting amongst themselves, Jacob looked at each of them and secretly blessed the Mother Mary for bringing these wonderful people together and into his life.

They were his family now.

Chapter 31

James

James had invited Lisa to walk in the park with him on Sunday. They had talked on Facebook and had seen one another at school, but technically this was their third date. James had finally talked to Lisa about his sister and Jacob, but he did not disclose how he met Jacob and Janet or anything about the vision.

"How's your friend, the old guy, doing now?" Lisa asked

"Really good. He had all his treatment and he is feeling fine. So everything is back to normal."

"That's great. You don't talk about your sister much. How is she doing?"

"Well, there is no change, really—she is just . . . there. Doesn't do anything, doesn't talk, just lies there. It is difficult to visit, 'cause you can't do anything . . . I don't how long she can go on like that. My parents don't really talk about it, and my mom is in this fantasy land where she thinks she is going to get better."

"You don't think she will?"

"No, I don't. Wow, that is the first time I said that. I have thought about it a lot but never said it out loud. It feels a bit weird to say it out loud. It's true, though, and it has to be said. No point pretending . . . Don't you just love the park? It is so magic sometimes."

Lisa stopped and looked at James. "You're different from other guys."

"Why do you say that?"

"Because you care about people and you like nature and you are just a nice, sweet guy."

They were standing close to one another. James leaned over and kissed Lisa gently on the lips.

James felt his whole body tingle. "Wow," he said and kissed her again, this time longer and deeper.

"I have an idea," he said as they broke apart.

"What?" Lisa was slightly breathless.

"Let's go to the aquarium."

"What?" Lisa stood incredulous.

"Let's go to the aquarium. We can look at the fish, dolphins and whales and stuff like that."

Lisa shook her head and smiled.

"You are different . . . Okay, let's go."

They held hands as they walked towards the aquarium entrance.

Chapter 32

Janet

Jacob was getting stronger every day. Janet knew she had to get back to her apartment and start looking seriously for a job. She had revelled in caring for Jacob. This was definitely a career she wanted to pursue. Janet wanted to look into registering for the upcoming semester in September. She was feeling so positive and happy. Her life was becoming more promising.

Jacob had said that she could stay as long as she wanted and there was no need to rush back. Janet felt very tempted but she had to start planning her next step, and Jacob needed to become more independent.

The moment Janet stepped back into her apartment, she knew something was amiss. She could hear someone in her bedroom. Instinctively, Janet picked up an umbrella and had one hand on the front door when her mother stepped out of the bedroom.

"Mother, what are you doing here? You scared me." Janet's heart was in her mouth.

"I might ask where you have been. I came to your apartment two days ago and there was no sign of you. I asked your neighbours where you were and they said you were looking after some old man." Janet's mother was angry, her posture stiff and unyielding.

"How did you get in here?" Janet was indignant. How dare she come in unannounced?

"When we got the apartment for you, I cut a spare key for emergencies. Since our last phone call, I have been trying to get a hold of you. I have left message after message."

"I just couldn't talk to you at that time—I was going through some stuff," Janet said defensively.

"Oh yes, your <u>real</u> mother." Janet's mother's whole body became rigid; she was tighter than a coiled spring.

Janet realized they hadn't moved. She was still at the front door and her mother by the bedroom. "Let's sit down and talk; I'll put the kettle on." As Janet made the tea, her mother sat primly on the couch, fiddling with her necklace and watch. Janet placed the tea in front of her mother and sat down in a chair opposite her, the mug of tea warming her hands.

"I haven't decided whether to contact this woman yet and I don't think of her as my mother, not at all. She just gave birth to me."

Janet' mother softened when she heard this. "I have heard horror stories about these women that contact their biological children, wanting money, recognition, things like that; or they have some illness and they need to ask for forgiveness—it is all based on selfishness."

"Yes, I have thought of that, and I haven't made a decision, so please don't stress about it and whatever happens, she will never be my *real* mother." Janet smiled at her mom and for the first time in a long time looked at her, really looked at her. She was an attractive woman for her age, well-dressed and immaculately made up; and her hair was done in the latest style. However, everything her mother stood for was based on appearances and materialistic values. Janet was hopeful that her mother had made a trip out here because she cared about her and her well-being, but there was something else, she sensed it.

"Did you come out here for another reason, besides seeing me?" Janet asked.

Her mother bristled. "Well, I wanted to make sure you were okay, and there is something else. Your brother is getting married." Janet's mother thinly smiled. "She is the daughter of an executive at the company where your brother works. They are a very wealthy family and influential in the community."

"Is Derek happy?" Janet knew the apple didn't fall far from the tree. Her brother was very superficial and self-centred.

"Of course he is happy. We all are. She is a lovely girl, and we would like you to come to the wedding."

"When is it?"

"In two weeks. I have to go back now and help with some last-minute arrangements and you can come out in a week's time. We will pay for your flight."

Janet looked at her mother incredulously. "You know I can't fly!"

"Oh, for heaven's sake, Janet, I thought you were over all that anxiety nonsense."

"Mother, it is not nonsense and, yes, I am a lot better at some things and I do want to fly someday, but I have to take it slowly, not be rushed into it."

"Why can't you just be nor— like everyone else. How am I supposed to explain this to Derek's new family? You are part of our family, Janet, and you need to be there."

"Is that why you left me here and moved to Ontario, so I could be part of the family? I am normal, Mother, but I am not your "normal." I don't know why I have these anxiety problems. Maybe it's genetic, which is something I may find out if I contact my biological mother, but I finished high school, I drive, even over bridges now, and I have worked and I have been looking after a very dear friend who has cancer—had cancer—and I went to all his appointments and sat with him in hospital and chemo, and I am going to go to college to become a care-aide and I have made great strides, but you can't expect me to go flying just like that . . ." Janet was rambling and close to tears.

"That is exactly what we expect. We got you this apartment and furniture; we pay your rent, and the least you can do is to be there at your

The Vision

brother's wedding." Janet's mother's eyes flashed with anger. She crossed her arms across her chest.

"I am sorry, Mother, sorry that I am a huge disappointment to you and sorry that you feel the way you do, but I can't do it and I won't."

"You get out of this apartment then and fend for yourself; maybe the old guy will put you up. I hope that is all it is, you helping some old man out and him not taking anything else from you."

Janet could not believe what she heard; she stood up and walked to the front door. She grabbed her purse. She couldn't face her mother but spoke to the door.

"I will be out of here in a week and then I will hand the keys in to the landlord. Tell Derek I hope he is happy and I hope his new wife isn't making a terrible mistake. Good-bye, Mother."

Janet shut the door quietly and then promptly burst into tears.

Chapter 33

Jacob

When Janet appeared at his door, in tears, so quickly after she had left, Jacob couldn't imagine what had gone wrong.

"Oh, Jacob, can I please come in?" Janet looked so vulnerable and he suddenly realized how young she was. She had been his support all these weeks and such a strong presence that he had come to think of her as far older than her years.

"Sit down, sit down. Whatever is the matter?" They both sat on the couch and Jacob held her hand as she cried.

When Janet felt more in control, she told Jacob the whole story of her mother's visit.

"She said a terrible thing about our relationship, Jacob. It made me feel sick."

"She is your mother, Janet; maybe she is just trying to look after your best interests," Jacob soothed.

"No, she is a bitch. I know I shouldn't say that about my mother, but she is. All she cares about is appearances and what looks bad, or how it reflects on her. She didn't even ask about how we met or that I have decided to become a care-aide, nothing... just that I had to be at my brother's wedding because I am his sister. I bet they don't even know I am adopted. I know she pays the rent, and after I had finished my training, I was going to get a job and start paying my own way. They are the ones that left me—I didn't ask them to move to Ontario. What does she expect?..." Jacob allowed Janet to carry on venting to get it all out of her system. When she stopped and took a breath, Jacob looked at her intently.

"Listen, you can stay here for as long as you want. I will pay for you to be my companion. You register at the college and we will go from there. Everything will be fine."

"Oh, Jacob, are you sure? I don't want to be a burden; I promise to not get in your way and we can set guidelines and, oh, I hope Simone is okay with this. You are still going to have Simone, aren't you? I know, you can give me free room and board for helping you or being your companion and that way you can afford to have Simone as well..." Janet was rambling and Jacob started to laugh.

"Stop with the verbal diarrhea already."

Janet blushed. "Sorry, I guess I was getting overexcited there."

"It's fine, we will think of something; anyway, what is important is that you have somewhere to live and you start your program and it will all work out."

Janet smiled gratefully and they sat in companionable silence for a while, before Jacob said, "I'm feeling hungry; how about rustling up something for us, hey?"

"Of course, I will see what you have in the fridge." Janet got up and went to the kitchen.

Jacob shook his head at the strange turn of events. He picked up Lorraine's picture.

"Now I have three women in my life: you, Janet and Simone. Not bad for an old man."

What Jacob had not counted on was Simone's jealousy. She was fine when Jacob was sick and had to go through chemo and lots of doctor's appointments, but now it seemed that Janet was stepping on Simone's toes by invading her territory. Jacob had known Simone long enough to immediately see the early warning signs. Janet was too wrapped up in her own worries and issues to sense the tension. Foolishly, Jacob tried to ignore it. "It will pass," he thought.

By the second week, after Janet had moved all her belongings into his small house, Simone's aura was a toxic red. He almost could see the flames shooting from her mouth. Simone was noisily making lunch with a few French swear words coming through. Luckily, Janet was out that morning to register for her course at the New Westminster College. She decided to take the sky train and see how long it would take her to get there and, based on that, plan her route to school.

Jacob walked into the kitchen, something he never usually dared to do while Simone was cooking or preparing food. Simone stopped what she was doing and glared at him.

"Let's have a coffee, Simone; take a break for a bit." Jacob reached over and put the kettle on.

"If we are going to have coffee, I want the proper stuff, not the crappy instant." Simone snapped the kettle off and gently pushed Jacob out of the way, so she could get to the coffee machine. Jacob put his hands up in mock defeat and went to sit at the kitchen table.

Simone slammed the cups down and sat down with a humph. No one spoke for the first few minutes. Jacob put his cup down and gently patted Simone's shoulders. She shrugged him off.

"Look, Simone, I know it is difficult for two women to share a kitchen and share household responsibilities."

Simone waved her hand and turned away in disgust.

"Janet got kicked out of her apartment. I would gladly let her stay here for free but she needs to feel she is doing something for me to pay for her room and board. Plus it is good for her resumé when she applies for jobs after she finishes her certification. Simone, I am not trying to replace you, no one could do that. I need you here, just as I need Janet here. You are both like family to me. Since I had the cancer, I have become so much more grateful to the wonderful people that surround me, such as you, Janet and James. Janet would never want to replace you, either; she knows how important you are to me and to her."

Simone's granite demeanour started to soften. She looked down at her cup. "I am getting older now, Jacob, and I need this job. You treat me well; some of my clients don't. You make it worthwhile coming to work every day; I would be devastated if I lost this job." Simone had tears welling up in her eyes.

"I would never let you go, not without a fight anyway"—Jacob smiled—"and besides, who would keep me in line, if I didn't have you?"

Simone brightened at this. "I have been acting like a jealous schoolgirl; I am sorry. I will apologise to Janet."

"No, there is no need for that. She is oblivious at the moment with all her other problems going on. Just show her the ropes and we will be fine." Jacob got up and stretched.

"I am feeling pretty good today; I think I will go out for a walk." Jacob got his hat and coat.

"Are you sure? What about lunch?"

"I won't be long, I have to go see . . . an old friend."

"Who is that?" Simone asked

"You don't know her; her name is . . . Mary. See you later." Jacob smiled as he shut the door. He realized he had one more important lady in his life.

Chapter 34

James

According to high school gossip, James and Lisa were now "an item." They didn't show any affection in school as such, but they definitely had their "mojo" going on. You could tell, by a look and a subtle touch, that they were more than good friends. James finally asked Lisa to the dance and she accepted without question. They spent time after school together, doing homework, walking in the park and sometimes watching TV together, usually at Lisa's house. (James was not allowed to have a girl in his house without a chaperone.) He felt comfortable with Lisa, and other than kissing and gentle petting, there was no urgency to go further, at least not yet. Lisa felt respected by this and appreciated his patience.

James met up with Janet and Jacob the Saturday before the dance. They all seemed in good moods, joking and laughing with each other. James had learned that Janet was living with Jacob and she was his companion. Janet also told him that she had registered for the care-aide course at Douglas College, in New Westminster, and would be starting in September.

"Wow, you are really going for it, aren't you?" James was impressed.

"Yeah, I need to do this and I really enjoy working with seniors."

"And she is good at it," Jacob retorted. "Now, young man, are you all ready for the dance tonight?"

"Yeah, it's no biggy; I'm just wearing jeans and a t-shirt. Lisa has some new dress or something; it's just a dance, don't understand what the big deal is." James looked embarrassed, but he was actually looking forward to it.

"Well, have fun and behave." Jacob winked at James.

"Hey, watch it, Gramps!" James playfully punched Jacob's shoulder.

The plan was to meet Lisa at her place and her dad would drive them to the dance. After the dance, James was to phone his dad and he would pick them up and give them a lift home.

James felt extremely nervous as he walked to Lisa's house. "Chill, man!" James shook his body out to release the tension. He rang the doorbell. Lisa's mom answered and asked him to come in. "You look nice, James," she said. James muttered a thanks.

"Lisa, James is here," Lisa's mom called out. Lisa came down the stairs. She had a short purple dress on with no sleeves; it was just low enough so as to not offend any parents or teachers. Her hair was loose with soft ringlets around her face. She had high heels on and a touch of makeup. James thought she looked beautiful. "Wow, Lise, you look good." He took her hand as she came towards him.

"Steady on there, James." Lisa's father had come in and mockingly chided James. James stepped back a bit and dropped Lisa's hand. They said their good-byes to Lisa's mom and went off in Lisa's dad's car. When they arrived at the school, Lisa got out first and Lisa's dad pulled James back. "Keep my girl safe and no monkey business, okay?"

"Yes sir." James was a little taken aback.

"See you at 11, Lisa, no later, yeah?"

"Yes, Dad, thanks for the ride. Bye." Lisa grabbed James' hand and started into the dance.

"Hope he wasn't too much," Lisa said.

"Nah, he is just being a dad."

The dance was a typical senior high school dance, with many attempts at bringing booze in and spiking the punch. Mickeys were planted in toilet tanks, behind curtains and in the bleachers. A lot were found but some remained hidden and a few kids got plastered. They were quickly kicked out with the threat of suspension. A couple already "three sheets to the wind" tried to come in but were promptly shown the door and barred for the rest of the dance.

James and Lisa had a great time, with lots of dancing and joking around with their mates. It was pretty hot in the gym and by 10 o'clock the air was stifling. James had a sudden urge to take Lisa to visit the vision site and explain all about it. "Hey, let's get out of here; we can have a walk through the park." James grabbed Lisa's hand and dragged her out of the gym.

"I want to show you something."

There seemed to be an urgency in James, and Lisa had to take her shoes off because she found it difficult to walk in them. Luckily it was a dry warm night. As they approached the site, Lisa pulled back. "James, I'm not sure I am ready for this." She looked up at him with a scared expression.

Suddenly James twigged. "Oh, Lisa, I am not going to . . . It's not that. I just want to show you something." James felt his phone vibrate in his pocket. "Hang on a minute." He took it out and read the text message. "Oh shit, we have to go back to the school; my dad just texted. He said there is something up with my sister." James grabbed Lisa's hand and they practically ran back to the school. He phoned his dad to pick them up. Neither of them spoke after that, Lisa unsure of what to say and James afraid of what his dad was going to say.

His dad was tight-lipped about it all, except that they had to go to the hospital straight away. Lisa kissed James on the cheek as they said good-bye and asked him to phone her when he could. "Sure, okay, talk to you later." They waited until Lisa got in safely and James' dad sped to the hospital.

James and his dad walked into Diana's room and found his mom sitting next to the bed, holding Diana's hand. There was every tube imaginable coming out of his sister, and it was clear that she was having difficulty breathing on her own.

"Mom, what's going on?" James' mother stood up and immediately hugged James to her chest and started crying. He let her cry for a while and then pulled away.

"What has happened?"

"Your sister, um , she has had respiratory failure, um, she can't breathe, and she is now on a ventilator . . . she needs a lung transplant; otherwise, she will . . . die . . ." James' mother sat down in the chair and covered her face with her hands. James' dad went over to her and put his hand on her shoulders.

"Do you think she will get one?"

"We don't know; they are looking for a match now." James' dad spoke, as his mother was too upset to speak.

James couldn't look at his sister—it didn't even look like her. She looked like some alien that was being hooked up for experimentation. He leaned up against a wall and slowly slid down until he was sitting on the floor. James didn't know what to do, so he just sat on the floor, listening to his mother crying softly and the respirator breathing for his sister.

James woke up with a start and felt a pain in his neck. He had been slouched over in an awkward position, dozing. He looked over at his sister and she was still there, breathing but not breathing. His parents weren't around, and he didn't know where they had gone. James moved his neck back and forth a few times to get the kinks out. He got up and went to stand by his sister. He decided to take her hand in his. It was so cold and limp that it didn't feel like it belonged to a living person.

"James." Someone called him and he looked at the door. No one was there.

"James, it's me, Diana." He looked at the corner of the room where he had been sitting. Enveloped in white light was his sister, Diana, standing and breathing on her own.

James dropped his sister's hand.

"James, you have to let me go. Turn off the machine. You have to let me go."

"Who are you? What is going on?"

"James, I need to live on the other side; this life is too painful for me. Turn off the machine."

"I can't do that, it is keeping you alive; they will get a donor . . ."

"It is too late for me, James. You need to do this for Mom and Dad. They can't do it, but you can."

"No, I can't. Diana, how are you there, when you are here." James pointed to the bed.

"James, I haven't been in that bed for a long time. I have been travelling to other dimensions, learning new and wonderful things. This life is not for me. I can learn and grow and then try again. I need to move on; the family needs to move on."

"No, I can't do it; it is not for me to do." James stepped away from the bed.

"James, I have seen your vision; I have seen Mary. She is waiting for me; she wants you to do this."

"You know about Mary?" James didn't understand what was going on.

"Yes, she is beautiful, kind and loving. She doesn't want me or anyone else to suffer. Can't you see you are all suffering, with me being this way?"

James scratched his head. His mind was racing, he couldn't think straight and all the time his sister, the one in the white light, was pointing to the ventilator and asking him to unplug it.

"Let me go, please let me go . . ." He could see his sister pleading with him. He looked at the lifeless body in the bed. Was that really his sister in that bed? He preferred to see the one standing, and speaking and talking about Mary and learning and growing.

Quickly, without any hesitation now, James went to the machine and pulled the plug. He pulled the mask off his sister's face. Nothing happened at first, and then there was a noise like a gurgling sound, a gasp and then nothing. No sound, just peace.

James looked at the vision of his sister in the corner. She was laughing and smiling.

"Thank you, James, oh thank you. Come and see me with Mary . . ." And then she disappeared.

James' parents walked into the room and saw the mask off and the noise of the ventilator gone.

"What have you done, James? Oh, my God, what have you done?" His mother ran to the bed and put the mask back on his sister, but she knew it was too late. They all knew it was too late.

James walked from the room. He had done what she had asked.

Although James was at peace with what he did, a lot of people weren't, including the hospital. They immediately brought in social services to assess the situation. James was not allowed to go home until he was questioned, psychiatrically evaluated and then debriefed. He stayed in a private room in the children's psych ward for a week. His parents were able to visit him but had to be accompanied by a psych nurse. James was savvy enough not to mention seeing his sister in the corner of the room talking to him or to speak about the vision of Mary. He knew he would be in for a long haul if he did. He just explained that his sister was suffering and she was going to die anyway. She needed to be able to die sooner than later and without all the bullshit in between. It was determined that James had a psychotic episode due to the strain of his sister's illness. He couldn't bear to see his sister suffering and, more importantly, what it was doing to his parents. The hospital didn't take it further and James was allowed to go home.

James wasn't able to have an intimate conversation with his parents in the hospital and he could feel the strain of his actions on both his parents. What surprised him was his father's gratitude for what he had done. This did not sit well with his mother, though.

"I have to be honest, James, I am grateful for what you did. I wish I had the courage to do it. It was inevitable that Diana would have died at some point."

"How can you say that, Kevin? We could have found a donor, she would have been able to live a normal life, we don't know what could have happened..." James' mother was not able to look at James throughout their conversation, as she was so angry at him.

"No, let's be realistic. Diana was gone a long time ago; she was not living, not really; she was existing, so let's not sugar-coat this."

"I can't believe that; she was there and she was going to get better. She just needed the chance."

"I don't fucking believe this." James stood up between them.

"James!" his mother said, shocked.

"Diana was dead, she is dead and now you are going to blame me for her dying. All my fucking life, everything revolved around Diana—getting her this treatment, hospital visits, hospital stays—you were never around for me. I had the most wonderful time of my life at that dance and then

I had to come back to the hospital and watch my sister breathe with the help of some fucking machine. Is that what life is all about? Do you think she wanted to be there? No, she didn't and someone had to do it, someone had to let her go . . . I didn't get to know her, I didn't even get to be her big brother. I was just another body in this family, not a real person . . . not a son, not a . . ." James started to break down and cry. His father got up and hugged him and they cried together. His mother went into her bedroom and shut the door.

The story leaked out from a hospital source and appeared in the *Province*. It read:

Brother kills sister in support of euthanasia

Vancouver hospital:

According to unofficial reports, a 10-year-old girl was euthanized by her 15-year-old brother. A young girl said to have the auto-immune disease Guillain-Barré was on a ventilator to assist her breathing while waiting for a lung transplant. She had the apparatus unplugged and taken from her by her brother, while the parents were having a well-earned break. It is unknown as to whether there was a donor available and how long the girl could have gone without succumbing to her disease. The brother said, "I couldn't bear to see her suffer, and what it was doing to my parents was worse." There appear to be no charges pending and the teenage boy has been released back home.

James had finished his exams for the year except for an English exam. Owing to the circumstances, the school would allow him to take the exam at home under supervision. James rejected this. He needed to get back to normality. Life at home was not good. No one spoke to anyone, not out of spite, but just due to not knowing what to say. Everyone was treading on eggshells. They could not yet plan a funeral for Diana because, owing to the extenuating circumstances of her death, an autopsy had to be performed.

James hadn't even seen Lisa. They had texted and talked on the phone but the conversations were brief. James couldn't go on his Facebook account because there was a lot of crap about his sister, both good and bad. A lot of people supported what James had done, but some didn't. He even got some threatening phone calls about how "he should be euthanized." James decided to go to school and do some cramming for his exam. He wanted to get away from the negativity in the house. He spoke with Lisa and told her he would meet her outside the school.

It was late in the school year, so thankfully there were fewer students than usual around. James could feel eyes boring into him as he walked through the schoolyard to the front entrance. Lisa was there waiting. She went up to him and held his hands and kissed him on the cheek.

"You okay?" she asked, concerned.

"Yeah. Let's go to the field and have a walk before we go in."

They held hands and walked to the sports field. It was relatively quiet.

"What a nightmare," James spat out.

"I know. How are you holding up at home?"

"It's awful, no one speaks to anyone, and we are all going around like zombies. I just wish we could bury my sister so at least that is done and we can kind of move on from there, you know? Not that we are going to forget her or what happened but at least that part will be finished.."

"James, I have to tell you something." Lisa dropped her hand from his and crossed her arms across her middle as though she were cold.

"What?"

"My parents don't want us to see each other until this all blows over."

"What? You can't be serious!" James was incredulous.

"This isn't me. We can still talk and stuff, but they are getting some weird phone calls and I am getting some flack from people, and it is, well, messy . . ."

"Do you think I did the wrong thing?" James stopped and faced Lisa.

"No, of course not, and I still want to see you. When school finishes, we can start to see each other again . . ." Lisa shrugged her shoulders. She had a pained look on her face.

"Fine, just fine. I guess we better get back for the bell." They walked back in silence but didn't hold hands.

Lisa promised to meet James outside the school after the first period. James went to the library to study. It was a waste of time—he couldn't study. He just doodled on his notes.

When the first period was finished, James stood outside waiting for Lisa. He waited and waited. Finally she showed up with a girlfriend, who gawked at James. He felt like some kind of weird celebrity.

"I have to study with Jenna; we have an exam tomorrow and I need to look at her notes."

"Right, okay, give me a call tonight."

"Yeah, sure, talk to you tonight." Lisa turned and walked away with her friend.

"This is bullshit," James said aloud. He started running and kept running. He could feel his adrenaline revving him up. With every pounding of his runners on the pavement, he was releasing all the pent-up anger he was storing. If he was in a race now, he would surely have won it. He got to the park and found his path; his breath was fast and stilted from his excursion.

He stopped in front of the altar. "Pleease, please . . . let me know I . . . did the . . . right thing." James could hardly speak from the running. He bent over to catch his breath, and when he got up, he saw the white light. Standing with Mary was his sister, Diana. She was holding her hand and they were both smiling at him.

James whispered, "Thank you." He began to walk slowly back to school.

Chapter 35

Janet

Janet and Jacob finally succeeded in speaking to James. They couldn't get through for a long time. They agreed to meet in their usual place on the following Saturday.

Janet took one look at James and she could see the damage all this was doing to him. She hugged him fiercely and he gratefully accepted her compassion. Jacob took him in a bear hug as well and James had to laugh. "You're pretty strong for an old man."

They sat down with their drinks and talked for a long time. James told them about seeing his sister and doing what she wanted and then finally getting the message that he had done the right thing from the vision of Mary and Diana.

Janet was in tears through most of it. "You are so brave, James—everything you have gone through, are going through. We are so proud of you." She put her hand on his hands and smiled through her tears.

"Thank you, that means a lot to me." James said gratefully.

"Would you do me a favour and come to the funeral when the time comes?" he asked.

"Of course," Janet and Jacob said in unison.

"We will do whatever we can to support you," Janet said.

When they parted ways, Janet and Jacob walked through the park for a bit.

"Do you think you will ever tell anyone about the vision, Jacob?" Janet asked.

"I don't think so. I think people have to find her out for themselves. You can lead a horse to water but you can't make it drink," Jacob said philosophically.

"Very true, Jacob, you are a wise man." Janet put her arm through Jacob's as they walked slowly home.

Janet couldn't stop thinking about James and what he was going through. It made her think of how lucky she was to have both James and Jacob in her life. Since her mother's disastrous visit, Janet refused to think of her family. She hadn't heard from her mother since and she knew that she wouldn't either. She had crossed the line and there was no going back now. She expected more from her father, but he was always forced to do whatever her mother wanted. Janet didn't think her father had an opinion of his own. He just did what he was told in return for a quiet life. "What a waste," she thought. Her father was an intelligent, kind man but spineless. As for her brother, he would do whatever it took to get ahead, including marrying someone he probably didn't love. "Well, good riddance to bad rubbish," Janet said aloud. She couldn't help but feel cheated somehow.

Janet had her mail redirected to Jacob's place and she received yet another notice from the ministry that her biological mother had requested to meet with her. They also stated that this was the last request she would make for a meeting. "What does that mean? She will no longer make attempts to meet with me?" Janet wondered. Maybe she was playing too hard to get. What would it hurt to just meet up with her? She wasn't going to allow her to barge into her life. They could just meet up and see where it goes. Janet couldn't help but have fantasies of meeting her *real* mother and them forming a bond and becoming the family that Janet yearned for. Against her better judgement, Janet phoned the ministry and got the telephone number to call her "mother." She didn't take up their offer of counselling and she didn't tell Jacob either. Somehow she knew he would disapprove.

The following week, Janet went to find a pay phone, which was not an easy task. She was smart enough not to use her cell phone or Jacob's land line. She eventually found one in a mall. Luckily, it was situated in a discreet area that allowed for privacy. Shakily, Janet put in the required coins and phoned the number. "Hello," a strong voice at the other end answered.

"Hello, is this Irene Thomas?" Janet asked. She couldn't stop trembling, and had to keep taking deep breaths to calm herself.

"Yes, who is this?"

"My name is . . . my name is Janet, Janet Wildwood."

There was silence at the other end.

"So you called; you decided to get in contact with me." The voice sounded accusing.

"Yes, it was a difficult decision; I am sorry I took so long." Janet was flummoxed—she wasn't expecting this response.

Irene softened a bit. "That's okay; sorry, I know it must be odd, me contacting you after all these years. I am, I am glad you did."

There was silence once more.

"Please insert another 25 cents please," the automated voice requested. Janet put in the coin and allowed it to drop before she spoke again.

"Would you like to meet up somewhere?" she asked.

"Yes, yes, that would be nice, good, yes." Irene sounded equally confused.

They arranged to meet for coffee in the mall she was in, next Friday.

"How will I know it is you?" Janet asked.

"I will be wearing a floppy hat; you don't see many people wear one, but that is my signature look." Irene laughed at this.

"Good, see you then." Janet hung up the phone quickly. She couldn't wait to get away from that area. She felt like a panic attack was coming on. She dived into the nearest restroom and locked herself in a cubicle. She sat on the closed lid of the toilet seat and put her shaking hands in her lap. "What have I done?" she groaned.

Chapter 36

Jacob

Jacob was concerned about Janet. She seemed preoccupied, almost secretive. Janet was pretty much an open book and, despite her insistence that there was nothing wrong, Jacob knew otherwise. He didn't want to press her—she would tell him in her own time. They had all been through so much, all three of them—James, Janet and himself. It was a wonder how a person could survive all these trials and tribulations. He knew he had help from the vision. Whenever he felt alone or that life becoming too much for him, he would either go to visit Mother Mary or think about her, and he would feel complete.

Jacob had his own preoccupation as well. He had gone for his regular blood test and seen the doctor for the results. Janet was unable to come with him, that day, so he went alone. The doctor spoke about his elevated white blood cell count. "We have to keep an eye on that. I am going to increase your dosage of the antiviral drug you are currently on. It may be that you just have caught a bug or a virus from somewhere. It would be a good idea for you to take it easy for a couple of weeks and come back for another blood test."

The doctor handed him another requisition for the test in two weeks time.

"But I am feeling so well; I don't feel like I have a virus."

"Well, that is good news; anyway, I am sure it is nothing to worry about. I will see you in a couple of weeks."

Jacob was not happy about this latest development, but he was going to keep it to himself. He didn't want to stay at home and worry, so he ignored the doctor's advice. He needed to go to the funeral of James' sister on Monday. He couldn't miss that.

Chapter 37

James

The hospital had finally finished the autopsy of his sister, Diana. The final diagnosis of death was respiratory failure. They also discovered that she had an enlarged heart, damage to her liver and other joint paralysis that was not detected before. It was deemed that if she had received a lung transplant, she would not have survived the procedure due to all the other complications her system presented.

This did not alter James' mother's view of him. Before she would not even speak to him, but now all she did was yell at him. Nothing he did was right. It was becoming intolerable to be in the same room as his mother. James didn't spend much time at home. He did a lot of walking through the park, cramming for his exam and shooting baskets at school when it was deserted.

The school counsellor suggested James get grief counselling but he said he wasn't ready yet.

He talked a lot with his dad, which he enjoyed. He hadn't had much of a relationship with his dad before, but his dad seemed to be making up for it now. They ate supper together and watched sports on TV and even went for drives. James' dad asked that James try to be patient with his mom, as she had been through a lot.

"Haven't we all been through a lot?" James said defensively.

"I know, but your mom had this fantastical idea that your sister was going to miraculously get better. I tried to tell her, the doctors tried; even I think Diana did in her own way. She feels she has failed. All this is so hard to understand, I have trouble with it myself."

James wasn't convinced. He could feel his mother's anger and, well, hatred towards him.

James was looking forward to closure with the funeral tomorrow.

The tiny church was full. There were family members, friends of the family and friends of Diana; teachers, doctors, nurses and, he was thankful, Janet and Jacob. They sat near the back so that Janet could have a quick exit if needed. Large crowds panicked her a bit.

James looked around at the faces, but they all swam before him. He was hoping to see Lisa among them, but she was not there. A couple of his buddies had come and he was grateful for their support. His mom had made a DVD of Diana's short life, and she looked painfully thin and pale in most of her images. There were a couple of shots of James as a small boy, holding his newly born sister and one of them at Christmas time, opening presents. He couldn't help but feel he was not part of this. It was all an act, the grieving brother. He had shed all his tears about her wasted life and knew that she was in a better place. They should be celebrating her newfound existence, not mourning the loss of a sad, pathetic young girl that had no life at all on this earth.

James watched the pictures, heard his sister's favourite pop songs and listened to some people speak about her courage, her faith and her love for her family. Neither his mom nor dad got up to speak and James didn't get up either. There were lots of tears by a lot of people—people who had barely known her, but maybe they were crying for his parents. She was buried in a gravesite on the North Shore, next to one of his grandparents. Supposedly there were plots available for the rest of the family. James knew it didn't matter where you were buried or cremated—it was more of a place for the living than the dead.

There were some sandwiches and beverages in the hall of the church after the funeral. James made himself as small as possible, crammed up against the back of the piano, so he didn't have to talk to anyone. Janet and Jacob spotted him and came to speak to him.

"It was a lovely send-off, James." Janet touched his shoulder.

"It was okay; I'm just glad it's over."

"Yes, you need to move on now," Jacob interjected.

"James, get out of there and come and speak to some of your relatives." James' mother walked determinedly over to James and glared at him. She looked daggers at Janet and Jacob, only because they were friends of James.

"We will be going now, James. See you on Saturday?" Janet asked.

"Wouldn't miss it for the world." James smiled back.

Jacob and Janet walked past James' mother and they could feel her hackles up, like they were some kind of predators.

"Poor James," Jacob whispered as he shook his head.

James took his final exam on the Wednesday and he felt he had done okay. He had passed it at least. He hadn't seen Lisa for a week now and the last time they spoke, it was awkward. James knew they were never going to see each other again. Oddly enough, he felt relief over it. Something in him had changed and, with it, the relationship had shifted. He still liked her, but it was more like friends than a couple. He had finished and passed grade 10 and he was looking forward to the summer and hanging out with his friends. He was contemplating getting a job to earn some money. He wanted to learn how to drive as soon as he turned 16 and he wanted to have the money to take lessons, so he didn't have to ask his parents for it.

He stayed away from home as much as possible and felt better when his dad got home from work; James didn't feel so alienated when his dad was around.

He came home just before six on the Thursday after the funeral. His mother was livid.

"Where have you been?" She had a plate of food in her hand.

"What do you mean? It isn't that late." James looked at her.

"I cooked supper for you and you don't even have the decency to come home on time and eat it."

"Well, that's a first; normally I have to get my own dinner."

"Why you ungrateful bastard . . ." His mother threw the plate at him. James ducked just in time and the plate hit the wall behind him. He started to laugh but his mother lost it and started throwing all kinds of dishes at him. Most of them missed him except a cup which hit him on the forehead and broke the skin.

"Mom, stop it . . . you're crazy . . . you hit me." James grabbed his mother's hands and held them down as she struggled to break free.

"Let me go, let me go!" She was screaming now. One of her hands broke free and she grabbed James' hand and bit his finger.

"What the hell!" James pushed her back into the counter where she cried out in pain.

"Why wasn't it you, why wasn't it you that died?" James' mother spat out the words and then her face crumpled and she started to cry. "Why did it have to be my little girl?"

James stared uncomprehendingly at his mother. Blood was coming out of his wound and running down into his eyes. He grabbed a kitchen towel and placed it on his forehead. Just then, his father walked through the door and stared at the macabre scene in front of him.

"What the hell is going on here?"

"Ask her, Dad. Ask her about who she really wishes was dead," James said menacingly.

"Karen, Karen, what did you do? What did you say?"

James' mother stopped crying. Tears mixed with her running nose dripped into her mouth, but she didn't wipe it away. "Yes, I wish it was James and not Diana. I am sorry, but I do. I can't help the way I feel . . ."

James turned away and shot out the door. He couldn't bear to see or hear any more. What he must have looked like, running down the street with blood pouring down his face, the towel wiping it every so often, and tears streaming down. He was getting funny looks but no one stopped him. They couldn't catch up with him for one thing, he was running so fast.

He made his way to the park and the familiar path. He lay on the ground near the altar, tucking his legs into a fetal position. He sobbed and sobbed until it hurt. He finally knew what his mother thought. She was not upset that he pulled the plug; she was upset that it was his sister and not him. James did not know he could feel so much pain. It felt like his heart had been ripped out. After what seemed like a long time, he felt empty; he had no more emotion in him to get rid of. The vision hadn't come to him and he wondered why. Why had she forsaken him as well? He sat up but couldn't make himself get up. He had no energy. He slumped back down and closed his eyes. He was asleep in no time.

James could feel something warm on his body, like the sun. He opened his eyes to the warmth, and a golden light embraced him. He didn't see the vision but he felt her warmth. He felt like he was being cocooned in her arms. She was comforting him physically. Gladly, he soaked up all the love and support she was giving him. He wasn't sure how long he felt her embrace but it seemed like a long time. It was long enough for James to feel energized again and whole. He got up after the light dimmed and realized he had slept there all night. He looked at his watch and it was 6:00 a.m. James made his way back to his house on autopilot. He didn't remember how he got there but he was standing at the front door ringing the bell.

His father answered, looking dishevelled, like he had been up all night.

"Where have you been?" He grabbed James into a hug and started to cry. "We called the police and they said they had to wait until morning to look for you and I phoned all your friends and everyone has been looking for you . . ."

"Dad, let me come in, I'm cold." Suddenly, James felt cold—he felt colder than he had ever been, and so thirsty. "I need a drink." James took a glass from the cupboard and he noticed all the mess had been cleaned up. He took a long drink of water from his glass and had to come up for air, he was drinking so fast.

"Steady, son. Come and sit down." James sat on the couch and started to shiver. His dad brought a blanket from the closet and placed it around him. "I think you are in shock." James' dad looked at his son, concerned. "I think we should go to the hospital. He looked at the dried blood on his forehead. "You probably should have had stitches."

"Where is she?" James asked.

"Your mother isn't well. I took her to the hospital. She has had a breakdown. James, she didn't mean those things she said."

"She did, Dad, she did. Please don't lie to me, I don't want to be lied to. I know she has felt that way. I've known it for a long time, but I didn't want to admit it."

"Ah, James, she is sick—"

"No, Dad, it's okay; I'm okay with it, really . . . I'm just really tired now. I think I'll go and lie down." James got up but he couldn't stay up. He fell back down to the couch and passed out.

Chapter 38

Janet

Friday had come so quickly. After the funeral, the rest of the week flew by. Janet could not concentrate on anything. Luckily, Jacob didn't seem to notice. He seemed a little drawn and pale. Jacob said he was feeling a bit under the weather, but he was fine. Janet scolded herself for not paying more attention to him and promised she would devote more of her time to Jacob after her scheduled visit with Irene.

Janet dressed in jeans and a pink, short-sleeved striped top. She wore open-toed sandals and had painted her toenails a bright red. She took time with her makeup and even blow-dried her short hair, something she never usually did. She made some lame excuse to Jacob about having to go to the college for further paperwork. Simone looked at her and smiled. "Someone is looking fashionable this morning."

"Are you sure you don't have a date?" Simone winked at her.

Janet blushed. "No, no, of course not . . . I have to go, see you later." Janet rushed out the door.

The Vision

The mall was busy and Janet hoped that they would be able to get a table that was fairly private. She was early, but as she was about to walk into the coffee shop, she saw her.

Irene definitely had her signature hat on. It was a floppy '70s-style hat, in an orange-red colour, with a bright yellow ribbon around it. She had on a long flowing dress decorated with a multitude of flowers on it, all different colours. On her feet she wore Doc Marten boots. She looked like a hippie-cum-bag lady. Janet was close to turning around and leaving, but she took a deep breath and went to the table.

Irene turned around and saw her. She stood up and embraced Janet. Janet could smell jasmine. It was oddly comforting.

"Well, look at you." Irene looked Janet all over. "You are a beautiful woman. Your parents must be proud."

Janet didn't say anything. She noticed that Irene had a herbal tea.

"I'm going to get a coffee."

"No, dear, let me. What would you like?"

Janet gave her order and Irene walked to the counter. She noticed that she had a bit of a limp.

Janet received her drink and they sat in an awkward silence. Janet could hear herself swallowing. Irene was staring at her with a big smile on her face. Finally she spoke.

"I have been waiting for this day. I am sorry if it felt like I was harassing you, but once I made the decision to try to contact you, I just couldn't wait to see you." Irene put her hand up and touched Janet's chin, moving Janet's face back and forth.

"You have my nose and mouth, but you have Ricky's eyes, sad eyes . . ."

Janet didn't say anything and looked intently at Irene's face. She was still youthful, and she had no idea how old she was. She did see a bit of familiarity with her mouth. It was small, with a full bottom lip and a thin top one. Her eyes were striking. They were a hazel colour, almond shaped and twinkly, like stars. There were a few lines around them but they were laugh lines.

They smiled at one another.

"Tell me about yourself, dear, and I will answer any questions you want to know about, well, about . . . whatever it is you want to know."

Janet didn't know where to start and she felt oddly protective of her adoptive parents. She didn't want Irene to know the difficulties she was having with them. Janet talked about where she grew up, and that she had a brother. She told her that she was going to college in the fall and that she looked after an older gentleman for the time being. Janet did not divulge her anxiety issues or where she lived or where her parents lived, for that matter. She felt it was way too early in their relationship to go into detail and Janet thought it was presumptuous to think that there might even be a relationship.

Irene listened intently. After it was clear that Janet had told her as much as she wanted to, Irene sat back. She fiddled with her napkin, looking down at the table. "I guess you'd like to know what happened and why you were adopted."

Janet surprised herself by saying, "Yes, I would like to know." She didn't think she was that bothered but now she couldn't wait to hear about it.

"Well. I didn't give you up, you understand; social services, or child welfare or whatever you want to call it took you from me."

Janet was shocked. She stiffened a bit.

"Honey, I didn't do anything to you, so don't think that. I loved you, but I was only 17 and not really equipped to be looking after a baby. Ricky and I were living on the streets, you see. We were living in one of those God-awful downtown eastside hotels. I tell ya, the streets were way cleaner and healthier than that dump. Cockroaches, rats, mould, you name it, it lived and grew there. After I found out I was pregnant, I told Ricky we couldn't live there anymore. I could have caught something bad. So we lived in the parks, the alleys. I always kept myself clean and healthy. Ricky would make sure I had all the food, even if he went without. When I had you, March 1, 1987, at 3:00 a.m., in the women's hospital, I took one look at you and fell in love.

I don't think I ever loved anything before that. I thought I loved Ricky, but the love I felt for you was all consuming."

Janet felt embarrassed by this proclamation, especially from a woman she didn't know.

"Well, I didn't have an address, no family to help look after me and you, so they took you away. I named you Skylark. I know it is a bird, but there was a band out at the time and they were called Skylark and they wrote this amazing song, called "Wildflower," which I loved.

Janet couldn't help but laugh. "I have one of the plainest names there is—Janet. I wonder what I would have been like if I had kept the name Skylark?"

Irene smiled at this too. She continued her story. "I never had any more children. You were my one and only. I couldn't have borne it if I had more and they were taken away too. Anyway, you seemed enough for me, even if I didn't have a chance to see you grow up." Irene's eyes started to well up with tears. Janet refused to allow her emotions to come into it. She didn't know Irene; she was hearing this story about her living on the streets and not wanting to give her up, and maybe that was all it was—a story.

Janet cleared her throat. "What is it that you want from me? I don't have any money, I am not sure what you expect from this . . ." Janet put her hands up to illustrate their situation.

"Oh, honey, I don't want anything from you; I don't deserve anything from you. I know you don't know me. I'm not expecting for you to become my long lost daughter. If this is the last time we see each other, I will be happy. I just wanted to see you, that's all." Irene smiled weakly, taking short breaths to stop herself from crying.

Janet softened. She found it difficult to *not* like this woman. She had a loving energy around her and seemed so genuine.

"I need to go now." Janet started to stand up. She was finding it difficult to keep herself in check and felt the need to go.

"Of course, I really appreciate you seeing me. Will you call again?" Irene looked so vulnerable and hopeful at the same time.

"I . . . think so, I need to . . . think about this. Is that okay?" Janet didn't want to give her false hope but she was afraid to dismiss her.

"That will be fine, dear, you think about it and hopefully we will talk again."

Janet hugged her briefly. Irene handed her an old brown bag.

"I want you to have this; it has been washed, so don't worry." Irene laughed.

"It was the only thing I bought for you before you were born, and I kept it. It was a blanket that I wrapped you in."

Janet couldn't look inside it; she whispered thank you and left. She had to get to the restroom before she fell apart. She closed the cubicle door and opened the bag. Inside was a small blue blanket with purple hearts on it. She buried her face in it and cried.

Chapter 39

Jacob

"You know, Jacob, I think our Janet has a boyfriend." Simone spoke as she served out their lunch. Simone had some time before her next client, so she decided to have lunch with him.

"Pwff." Jacob made a face of disbelief as he sat down with Simone.

"Have you noticed how preoccupied she is and—" Simone emphasized the *and*—"she is not as attentive to you as before."

"No, I have not," Jacob grumbled.

"Did you see how she looked this morning? Like she was going out on a date, huh, huh?"

"So what if she does? It's her business." Jacob couldn't help but feel a bit jealous. He had been worrying about his own health but he did notice Janet's evasiveness.

"Just commenting, that's all. Don't get yourself all riled up." Simone liked to push Jacob's buttons.

The phone rang. Simone got up to get it.

"Hello, this is Jacob's house." Jacob rolled his eyes. Simone always answered with this phrase.

"Yes, just one moment." Simone passed the phone to Jacob. "It is James' father; he wants to speak to you.

Jacob took the phone. "Hello, this is Jacob."

Jacob heard about James going missing and then coming home and how he was now in hospital from shock and dehydration. "James wanted me to let you know, because he said you had some kind of meeting or get-together tomorrow," James' dad said.

"Yes, we usually get together with Janet on Saturday morning. Is he going to be all right?" Jacob asked, concerned.

"Yes, he will be fine. He should be out of hospital by this evening."

"Would it be all right if we come to visit him at home on, say, Sunday?"

"I'm sure he would like that. I will get him to call you when he gets home. One more thing: James' mother is in hospital too; she had a breakdown from all the stress of our daughter's illness and . . . death."

"Oh, I am so sorry; your family has been through enough." Jacob was mortified.

"She said some terrible things to James. She didn't mean them, she's sick." James' father suddenly went silent.

"Please, don't trouble yourself with the details, we will wait to hear from James, and please give him our love. Take care of yourself as well." Jacob hung up and shook his head.

"That poor family. So much grief." Jacob explained what had happened. Jacob silently chided himself for being a jealous old man over something so trivial as Janet having a male friend.

Simone left after lunch and Jacob settled down to his crosswords. He wasn't in the mood for a walk today, as he was feeling fatigued and slightly depressed. He couldn't stop thinking about James and his family. He also kept thinking how lonely he would be when Janet eventually went. He was getting too dependent on her. She was a young woman—she should be out enjoying herself, not stuck here with an old man. He needed to get back to the seniors' centre and start getting involved with people his own age. Jacob vowed he would start back to the seniors' centre next Monday, and the food bank too. "Enough of this self-pity," he said aloud.

Janet came through the door at three o'clock. She looked dreadful. Her face was swollen from crying.

"Janet, what has happened to you?" Jacob got up and drew her to a chair to sit down.

"Oh, Jacob, I should have confided in you. I wish I had. I am so confused . . ."

Jacob noticed that Janet was fiercely holding an old paper bag. Janet took out the small baby blanket and passed it to Jacob.

"Why do you have this?" he asked her.

"My biological mother gave it to me. Her name is Irene." Through some tears, Janet explained how she had contacted her biological mother and the meeting they'd had together. She gave him the details of her appearance and what she had said.

"The idea of coming from the street, seems so, so horrible, and having a homeless teenager as your mother. The way she dressed, as well . . . I have no idea what kind of place she lives at. She does live somewhere because I have her phone number and she isn't dirty or anything—she actually smelled like flowers—and she kept referring to this Ricky, who I assume is my father, I mean, biological father." Janet paused. "But I like her Jacob, I think she is genuine and she does have this feeling for me, but I don't know, I am not sure what I want to do about her."

"Janet, you don't have to do anything, not yet anyway. Just absorb what has happened and take it slow. Don't rush into anything. You have the power to contact her again or not; it is your choice, not hers. Would it be a good idea to see someone, one of those counsellors you told me about, to discuss this? They could advise you."

"Yes, you're right. I . . . you are so sensible and . . . what would I do without you?" Janet came over and kissed Jacob on the cheek.

"I was thinking the same thing about you." He smiled.

"Now, I have to tell you about James." Jacob told Janet about the phone call and they confirmed together that they would visit him on Sunday.

Janet went to lie down. Jacob shook his head. "Life is never dull." He put the crossword down and closed his eyes. He decided to have a nap as well.

Chapter 40

James

James was glad he didn't have to stay in hospital for long. It held a lot of bad memories. He took it easy for the next two days and, that afternoon, Janet and Jacob were coming to visit. He was glad about that. His father was very attentive and he let James be for the most part. He did talk to him about seeing a counsellor or therapist. The doctor suggested one that specialized in grief and was good with teens.

"I don't know, Dad. I'm kind of done with talking right now. I just want to get a summer job and chill with my friends."

"You can still do that, but it would be good for you to talk to somebody about what has happened, how you feel. I am going to see someone; we have all been through a lot. Promise me you will think about it, yeah?"

James nodded his head and his dad left him alone. He watched a movie to take his mind off things until Janet and Jacob arrived.

They sat in the living room and his dad said he had to go out for a while.

"Your dad is a very nice man," Jacob said approvingly.

"Yeah, he is pretty decent. I never really talked to him much before but we have gotten really close, since my sister . . . since she has gone."

Janet crossed her legs and tried to relax, but she found it difficult. She knew James had been through some pretty bad stuff. "What happened, James? Why did you run off?"

James began the whole sorry story of his mother's meltdown and her confession. There wasn't any emotion in James' voice except when he spoke about being embraced by Mary.

"It was so wonderful, I can't really describe it. Just that she was there for me, and all the hatred my mother had for me was taken away by her presence."

Jacob and Janet sat mesmerized by James' tale.

"You know, I don't want to go see my mom, don't want to talk about her, but I do feel sorry for her. She lost someone that means more to her than her husband and son."

Janet thought of Irene when he said that. She cleared her throat to stop the emotion that was building up. "What are you going to do now?" she asked.

"Like I told my dad, I am going to get a job, chill and just see what happens."

"What about Lisa?" Jacob asked.

"Ah, it didn't work out. No biggy—just like you said, Gramps, there are many fish in the sea."

They all laughed at that.

"Anyway, how have you two been? Anything new?"

"Well, I have met my biological mother," Janet said

"What!"

Janet told James about her meeting with Irene. She didn't go into too many details and didn't tell him about the blanket.

"Are you going to see her again?" James asked

"I don't know yet. I think I am going to speak to a counsellor and sort out my feelings first."

"My dad wants me to see someone like that."

"It would be a good idea, James," Jacob interjected.

"Yeah, maybe. How about you, Gramps, feeling okay?"

"As well as what can be expected for an old geezer like me." Jacob wasn't exactly lying.

James' dad came through the door, and Janet and Jacob got up to leave.

Janet gave James a hug and Jacob squeezed his shoulder.

"See you next Saturday, okay?" Janet asked.

"For sure." James said good-bye to them at the door.

He came and sat down in the living room. James turned to his dad.

"I think I will take you up on that offer to see someone."

His dad smiled. "Glad to hear it, son, glad to hear it."

Chapter 41

Janet

Janet sat down in the counsellor's office. It was a small room but brightly lit with lots of pictures of positive affirmations, such as "you are beautiful, inside and out"; "blessings of love and light to all" and "treat yourself as your best friend." Next to the two-seater couch was a small dog bed with a little cock-a-poo snuggled deeply inside it. The counsellor introduced herself.

"My name is Sue." Janet held her hand out. "Mine is Janet. Nice to meet you."

With the pleasantries over with, they both sat down. "I hope you are okay with dogs; this is Maggie, my therapy dog. She is hypoallergenic and very sweet."

"I love dogs. I think it is wonderful to have one in a counsellor's office." Janet smiled.

Sue had a kind and open face with very expressive hands, which she used a lot. She had been recommended by the ministry's office.

"Now, I know a little bit about your situation and from what you explained to me over the phone." She looked down at her notes. "So, your biological mother, Irene, has contacted you and you met her once, is that right?"

Janet nodded yes.

"What was your first impression of her?"

"Well, to be honest with you, when I first saw her, I thought she was a flake, if that is the right term. Kind of hippie-ish, eccentric. I almost didn't go in to meet her. I thought, 'What have I gotten myself into?' Then I met her and found she was very sweet and seemed nice. She said she didn't want anything from me, except to meet her. She told me that I was taken from her by the ministry because she lived on the street. She also spoke about a Ricky, who sounds like he might be my father." Janet had brought the blanket with her and took it out of the paper bag. "She gave me this blanket." Janet became very emotional and couldn't help the tears that started to fall. Almost on cue, Maggie jumped up and sat beside Janet and nuzzled her nose into Janet. Janet smiled. "Did you teach her how to do that?"

"No, as a matter of fact, she is very intuitive and just senses when people need her. She is a great asset to have around."

Janet continued as she petted the dog. "This blanket was the one that she wrapped me in, apparently, before I was taken away. I mean, my guard is up—I don't want her to come into my life and mess with me, you know what I mean? I haven't got a good relationship with my adoptive family, so I am, well, very confused..."

"There are a few things that you have to do before you meet this woman again. If you do in fact meet this woman again. One is to set boundaries for yourself. You said that your guard is up, which I believe is very important. Regardless of whether Irene had to give you up or not, she did not bring you up. She gave birth to you and that was as far as it went. All your values, your learning, came from your parents, family and environment. You don't owe this woman anything. I know that may sound cruel, but it is true. The ball is in your court. You can set the type of relationship you want. The blanket, whether Irene meant to or not, was a bit of blackmail. It set you spinning and thinking about 'what if...?'"

"Yeah, I have been thinking about a lot of stuff lately and wondering what my life would have been like if Irene had brought me up. There is one thing: I have a lot of, well, anxieties and phobias, and I am pretty sure Irene does, or did, and maybe even my biological father, who I know nothing about. Is it genetic?"

"There is a good possibility there are some genetic factors involved, but it depends on the environment you grew up in, how safe you felt—there are all kinds of variables. I wouldn't go into it too deeply. You are what you are. From what I understand, you are making great strides in dealing and coping with these issues. You seem to have strategies and you know how to use them." Sue smiled kindly at Janet.

Janet felt a tinge of pride at this realization.

"The second thing is to not let your current relationship with your adoptive family allow you to use Irene as a pawn against them. That would be unfair to Irene, and to your family."

"I know, I feel like I want to shove the fact that I have contacted Irene in their faces," Janet admitted, ashamed.

"That is perfectly natural. You are human and your family have treated you badly, so your natural instinct is to hurt them back. However, that can backfire and it tends to end up with you feeling worse about the whole situation. Before you take your next step, you need to feel you are safe, and by that I mean, you have to feel secure in yourself and environment. I read that you like to do yoga?"

"Yes, I love it." Janet confirmed.

"Yoga is great for grounding and taking you out of your head. Carry on and do that and spend time with your friends, doing the things you love. That way, when you are ready to make a decision about seeing Irene, it will be made when you feel safe and confident in yourself. There is no rush. Irene didn't contact you until now, so you can take as long as you want to meet her again."

Janet sighed deeply. "You're right. I don't feel I can make a good decision at the moment. Thank you, I will wait until I feel like I can make the right decision for myself."

"There is one more thing. I love positive affirmations and I am a great believer in what they can do." Sue took a card from one of the shelves off the bookcase.

"Please take this and say it to yourself every day."

The card read: "Harmony and peace, love and joy surround me and indwell me. I am safe and secure."

"I love Louise Hay and she is the queen of affirmations, as far as I am concerned. This is one of her affirmations. This will help you by saying it and really feeling it every day."

"Thank you, Sue. I will do that."

They agreed to see one another again, once Janet made a decision as to whether she would see Irene. Janet petted Maggie once more and thanked Sue again.

Once out of the office and walking down the street, Janet decided to see what yoga class she could take for that day.

Chapter 42

Jacob

Jacob got back to volunteering at the food bank and going to the seniors' centre once a week. He was feeling better, not 100 percent but better. He didn't bother with the blood test the doctor suggested he take. He felt the increase in the medication was what he needed.

He was glad to see that Janet had made an appointment with the counsellor and that she felt better about the whole issue surrounding her "real" mother and her adoptive family. Janet said she wasn't ready to see Irene again; she needed time and distance before she made the decision. Jacob felt proud of Janet and all that she had been through and how she was coping.

"What a trooper," he said to Simone. Simone agreed that she was a special kind of person.

Jacob decided to go to the seniors' centre by himself that afternoon. Janet had offered to go with him and play bingo or shuffleboard. But Jacob felt the need to be by himself, so he said he would take the bus and she could pick him up around 5:00 p.m.

The day was warm and he took off his jacket as he waited for the bus. He was surprised how tired he got after the short walk to the bus stop. He was glad when the bus pulled up and he sat down near the front. Jacob felt tightness around his chest and it made him uncomfortable. He loosened his shirt by undoing the top button. That eased it a bit. When he got off the bus, Jacob found himself wheezing as he climbed the few stairs to the centre. He needed a drink of water and to sit down. He made it to the cafeteria and got himself a drink from the water cooler. Jacob could feel that his breathing was constricted. He forced himself to take deep breaths, to slow his heart rate down. This helped. The breathing became better and the tightness eased. "Silly old fool," he muttered to himself. Jacob sat for a few minutes and then made his way to the hall to play bingo. He enjoyed himself among his friends. Janet came in to pick him up and found him chatting to Lilly, one of the oldest members of the seniors' centre.

"Hello, Lilly, how are you?" Janet inquired.

"As good as can be expected. I will be 92 next month, you know." Lilly was very proud of her age and the fact that she still came to the centre every day.

"I know, you are marvellous," Janet complimented her.

"Lilly gives me hope." Jacob winked. "I want to be just like her when I reach that age."

They all laughed. When Jacob got home, he felt exhausted. It was all he could do to sit and have supper. They sat down after supper to watch TV. Jacob fell asleep after half an hour and started snoring. Janet gently woke him up.

"Jacob, you need to go to bed, you are falling asleep." Jacob didn't protest and stumbled off to bed. Janet continued to watch TV until ten. As she as getting ready for bed, she could hear Jacob coughing. Maybe he was coming down with a cold.

Chapter 43

James

School had officially finished and James was glad to be out of there until September. He applied to some local restaurants for jobs as a busboy or dishwasher. He knew they were crappy jobs but he had to start somewhere. James started playing basketball with some of his friends and they played once a week at the school court. He even started running the track; it felt good when he was running, and he even thought he might try out for the track team next year. His friends didn't talk to him about what had happened with James' sister and James didn't tell them about his mom being in hospital. He just wanted to get back to some kind of normality.

James agreed to see a counsellor, but the first one he saw turned out to be brutal. He didn't seem to understand James at all and kept going on about why James felt he had to play God and switch off the machine. James told his dad he wasn't going to see that jerk again. His dad persuaded him to see someone else. This counsellor was young and worked with at-risk youths in the downtown eastside, but he also specialized in grief counselling. James didn't really care what his qualifications were, as long as he could just talk and not be criticized.

They met in the park, as this counsellor didn't like working in an office. He agreed to meet him outside the aquarium. James couldn't help but think about Lisa and their first kiss nearby.

A tall skinny guy with spiky hair loped his way towards James. "You can't be serious, man," James said to himself. He looked like he was twenty.

"Hey, I'm Greg, and you must be James." Greg held out his hand and James was surprised at the firm handshake.

"Let's stroll." They started to walk on the seawall.

"So, what do you like to do?" Greg asked James.

"Uh, basketball, ice hockey in the winter and I like to run."

"Nice, I like running myself. I tried basketball but I'm too clumsy." He laughed at himself.

"What kind of shows and movies do you like?" They talked for a bit about what was good at the movies and what TV shows they liked. They reached the concession stand at Second Beach and Greg bought James a pop and he had an ice tea. They sat on a bench under the trees by the playground.

"So, James, how are you feeling these days?"

"Okay, I guess. Well, not great, you know. I guess you know what has been going on?"

"Yeah, I had a chat with your dad—seems like a nice guy."

"Yeah, he's been great."

"But your mom has not been so great?"

"No, no, she, uh . . ." James didn't know what to say.

"It seems to me like the Universe has thrown you a curve ball."

"What do you mean?"

"Well, first your sister dies, then your mom dumps on you. Not the best scene in the world, yeah?"

"No, pretty shitty. I mean, pretty bad."

Greg laughs. "Don't worry about the swearing, I can swear with the best of them."

"Do you believe in anything, James?" Greg asked.

"I don't know what you mean?"

"I'm not talking about religion, 'cause a whole lot of damage can be caused in the name of religion. I'm talking about God, Jesus, Allah, Buddha—just someone or something higher than yourself, or even your higher self."

"What is your higher self?"

"It is you without ego, without judgement, judging yourself and others—the you that can love yourself and others unconditionally."

James thought about that and then remembered the vision, Mary. "Yeah, I do have someone."

"That's great. It really helps to have someone or something to call upon to ask for help or just be there for you when you need it. Like the Beatles said, 'I get by with a little help from my friends.'"

James laughed. He liked this guy. "Hey, do you feel like going for a run?" James asked Greg.

"Yeah, sure, no racing, though. I doubt I'm in your league." They both got up and started running towards the seawall.

Chapter 44

Jacob

Jacob was not well. He felt exhausted. His breathing was constricted and now he had this cough that kept him awake most nights. He refused to go to the doctor despite Janet's and Simone's nagging. He tried to convince himself that he just had some kind of flu or cold. He got Janet to get him some over-the-counter cold/flu medication, but the relief he got from that was minimal. Jacob found it difficult to eat anything except soup. He didn't have an appetite but he knew that he was setting off alarm bells by not eating, so he pretended to be hungry. Apart from the soup, Jacob would somehow get rid of the rest of his meal, either in his napkin or in the washroom down the toilet, or throw it out in the garbage when no one was looking.

Jacob dozed most of the time and would then wake himself up with the coughing. He had the TV on constantly, not because he was watching it, but because he wanted to avoid talking to Janet and Simone. He didn't want to get involved in a fighting match about whether he should go to the doctor.

Janet gave him the ultimatum that if he didn't feel better by the end of this week, he was going to see a doctor, "no ifs, ands or buts."

Jacob needed to go to the washroom. He had refused help before but didn't think he would make it on his own this time.

"Janet, can you help me to the washroom please?" Jacob called out. There was no answer. Janet must be in her bedroom. He called louder, "Janet." The strain on his voice made him cough. He couldn't stop and his lungs felt like they were going to explode. He had to sit down again. He felt like he was fighting for his breath. Janet finally came running out of her bedroom. Jacob had started to vomit with the acceleration of coughing and Janet could see there was blood in the vomit. She picked up the phone and dialled 911.

Chapter 45

Janet

Janet's back hurt from sitting in the hard-backed chair for so long. She had been waiting for a couple of hours to hear back from the doctor. Jacob was having various tests to determine what was going on. He was just being wheeled back into the room after getting a cat scan. The nurses had administered some kind of pain relief and Jacob was feeling dopey from it.

Janet held his hand after the monitors had been reattached. He smiled weakly at her.

"Why don't you have a little sleep now, you must be tired," she prompted Jacob. Jacob didn't say anything and closed his eyes. Janet looked at the drawn, pale face with the five o'clock shadow that was now visible. Jacob was gently snoring as he finally slept peacefully. She suddenly felt a surge of love for this wonderful old man. Fate had brought them together and changed her life. Janet laid her head on the side of the bed while holding his hand. The next thing she heard was the sound of the nurses checking Jacob's vitals.

"Ouch." Janet's neck cracked as she sat up from the awkward position. Jacob was still asleep. Janet rubbed the back of her neck and moved it back and forth to regain its mobility.

"It is getting late; why don't you come back tomorrow morning. We will know more in the morning as the test results come in and the doctor has a chance to look at them. He will probably sleep for quite a while." The nurse motioned towards Jacob.

"Yes, I guess you're right. What is the best time to come in?"

"The doctors make their rounds about 8:00 a.m., so between 8:00 and 8:30."

"If he wakes up and is in any way distressed, please call me." Janet looked earnestly at the nurse.

"Of course, we have your number, but everything will be fine." She smiled kindly at Janet.

"Thank you." Janet made her way out of emergency to her car. She made the wise choice of following the ambulance. Janet went home and set the alarm for 6:00 a.m. She had a hard time sleeping, thinking about Jacob, James, Irene and her family. Her mind didn't shut down until about 4:00 a.m. When the alarm went off at six, Janet got up, showered and had a light breakfast. She pulled out the card that Sue had given her and read the positive affirmation to herself. She drove to the park and, because it was early, found a free parking spot in one of the nearby streets. Janet walked to the bush and picked up the pink runners. She put them on and walked the short distance to the path. Janet approached the altar, got on her knees and bent her head in prayer.

"Mother Mary, please help me through this difficult time. I need some guidance and support. I don't have a good feeling about Jacob's illness and I'm confused about whether to continue to see Irene. I am also concerned about James and all that he is going through. Please give me the strength and courage to face it all. I would really appreciate that." Janet knelt for what seemed like a long time. She could feel the heat of the light on her shoulders. She opened her eyes and saw Mary standing before her with outstretched arms. Janet lifted her own arms up, reaching towards Mary. She could feel an electric current of healing energy come into her. It vibrated all the way up through her arms and moved all through her body. It finally settled in

Janet's heart. The wave of energy slowed, pulsed gently and subsided. The light faded and Mary was gone. Janet got up off her knees and strode with a newfound purpose and strength back to the bush and returned the runners. She breathed in the fresh morning air as she walked back to her car. Janet then drove to the hospital.

Chapter 46

James

James got a job as a busboy-cum-dishwasher in a local Italian restaurant. He started working four evenings a week, Thursday through Sunday. It was minimum wage but he did get a meal each evening and a percentage of tips. It was grotty work but he liked the staff and the food was incredible. It certainly made school more appealing. James also could ride his bike to and from work, which made him more independent. He got home late one night from his shift and found an envelope addressed to him, left on his nightstand. He opened the letter and read it. It was from his mom.

Dear James,

I am writing to you because I know you don't want to see me at this time. If I was you, I wouldn't want to see me either. I have not been the mother to you that I have wanted to be. I pretty much put you last in trying to look after your sister for all these years. I realize now that I took you for granted and you were made to fend for yourself through a lot of your growing up. I truly wish that I could erase the past. I am so sorry for all the hurtful things I said to you and for the way I treated you. I am asking you to find it in your heart to forgive me and allow me a second chance. I know it is not going to be easy and this is one of the steps I have to make in my road to recovery, I have a long way to go. Please know this, I do love you and I always will.

Love,

Mom

James reread the letter several times. He knew it was late but he called Greg's number and left a message asking if he could see him as soon as possible. James got undressed and put the letter under his pillow. He fell asleep and dreamt about his mom.

Greg met James in the park the next day. It was raining and colder than it had been for a long time. James zippered his rain jacket up and put up his hood. They walked along the seawall for a while and then decided to go to a local coffee shop on Denman. It was crowded but they managed to find a table. James pulled out the well-worn letter from under his jacket and handed the letter to Greg. Greg read it and whistled. "Wow, that is some letter. What do you think about it?" He handed the letter back to James.

"I'm not sure, I'm totally confused. It was easier for me to hate her after what she did and said, but now . . ." James held up his hands.

"The way I see it, James, is that you need to do a couple of things here to move on from this."

"What's that?"

"First you have to find a way to forgive your mom. I'm not saying you forget what she did, but it will be better for you to be able to forgive her. This doesn't mean you run to her with open arms and make like a sappy TV commercial." James smiled at this. "But that is the first step to repairing your relationship with her. The second thing you need to do is to forgive yourself."

"Why, what did I do?" James asked.

"You survived, your sister didn't. There is something called 'survivor's guilt.' When people are involved in accidents or traumatic situations and someone dies, the ones that are left holding the bag, as it were, can feel tremendous guilt and pressure that they survived. Why were they spared, why didn't they succumb to whatever happened? How can they possibly justify their right to life when the other ones were denied it? That is a pretty heavy load to bear and that is what you are up against."

"Holy shit, is that why I feel so crappy—I mean, besides the way my mom treated me?"

"Yeah, but you can start to diminish that load by forgiving yourself. Cut yourself some slack and instead of condemning, give yourself a pat on the back. This world is a beautiful place, but it's also a difficult one and it takes guts to live it to its full."

James sat back. "Huh, I guess you're right. When I was little, I used to think that if I got sick, I would get more attention. The trouble was that I was a terrible faker. My parents saw through it every time. I might as well tell you now, I used to smoke pot all the time. It helped to dull the pain for a while. The only trouble was that I started to need more and more of it to have the same effect. I even took, well, stole some money from my mom's purse to buy it. She was too busy with Diana's sickness to notice. Anyway, I stopped smoking it and I am pretty sure I won't go back to it. I have some of that faith you were talking about. She helps me to feel better . . ."

Greg smiled at James. "You're an old soul in a young body, you know that, man? You are experiencing some life-altering stuff that not everyone has a privilege to go through. You are going to be just fine, better than that, you are going to be amazing. I feel pretty blessed to know you."

James couldn't help blushing at this heartfelt proclamation.

"How did you get involved with the counselling stuff and working with addicted kids?' James was truly interested.

"I won't go into details but just to say I know a little bit about what you and some of these kids are going through. Hey, the sun has come out—why don't we go shoot some baskets? I have a ball in my car." Greg playfully tagged James on the shoulder. "First to 12 has to buy lunch."

"You're on!" They walked out and finished their session over hoops and a Subway.

Chapter 47

Jacob

Jacob felt like he was only partially there. He was given so much morphine, it was like he was floating around in space. It was hard to stay grounded. Janet was still by his side, trying her best to cajole him into eating and drinking something. They were waiting for the doctor to come by to tell them what was going on.

Janet had slipped out and phoned Simone to tell her what was going on. She said she would go to the house and do some casseroles to freeze and she would then come by the hospital later on. As she walked back to the room, a doctor whom Janet had not seen before was speaking to the nurse outside Jacob's cubicle. The nurse saw Janet and introduced her to the doctor. "This is Dr. Clancy; he is a cancer specialist for the hospital."

Janet's heart sank as she heard cancer. "Can we talk somewhere private?" he asked Janet. She nodded yes and he ushered her to a spare room that was vacant.

"I am afraid it is bad news. I understand Mr. Schroeder had colon cancer some months back"— the doctor reviewed his notes—"and the cancer was successfully removed, is that right?" Janet found it hard to find her voice, but she muttered, "Yes."

"Well, it has spread to his lungs and it is a very aggressive form of cancer that is in the later stage, so in other words, stage 4. It also appears to have spread to some of his lymph nodes and we also suspect it is in his liver. In other words, it is terminal."

Janet couldn't help but gasping, she felt the room start to spin and closed her eyes to stop it.

"Are you okay?" the doctor asked, concerned.

Janet kept her eyes closed and willed herself to get a grip. She opened them when she felt the doctor taking her pulse. She let him finish and said more forcefully than she wanted to, "I am fine, I am okay, it was just the shock of hearing about the . . . the . . . cancer." She felt the blood rush back to her face as she stood up. "What happens now?"

"We really need to get him to the cancer clinic for internal radiation, to make him more comfortable, and then he and you, I guess, his family, have to decide about the palliative care."

"How long does he have?"

"It's hard to say . . . maybe two to three months, maybe sooner. I am sorry . . ." The doctor looked at her compassionately.

"It can't be easy," Janet said.

"I'm sorry?"

"It can't be easy telling people that they haven't got long to live . . . It must be difficult."

"No, it isn't easy, but I am afraid it is a part of the job. Shall I come in with you to speak to Mr. Schroeder?"

"No, it's okay, I will do it, thank you anyway." Janet walked into Jacob's cubicle and pulled the curtains around the bed. She sat down on the chair and took Jacob's hands.

"Jacob . . ." Janet started.

"Janet, you don't have to say anything, I know. I know I am dying. I have known for a while."

Janet couldn't say anything. She just held his hands.

"I would like to go home for a while, and then when it gets too much, go to the hospice or wherever is easier. I don't want to make it difficult for you and Simone."

Janet managed to find her voice. "You have to go to the cancer clinic for some kind of radiation to make you more comfortable and then I will see about bringing you home." Janet's face was wet with tears.

"You know, since Lorraine, you are the best thing that has happened to me."

Janet shushed him. "Don't talk anymore, it's tiring you out."

Jacob closed his eyes and whispered, "Don't tell Simone I said that."

Janet couldn't help but smile.

Jacob was transferred to the cancer clinic and stayed there for a week. The radiation helped somewhat and Jacob felt a bit stronger. Among Janet, Simone and the social services, it was decided that Jacob could go home as long as Janet and Simone could care for him. They were given a commode on loan, a walker and a wheelchair. A community nurse came once a week to check on Jacob and advise Janet on how to ease bedsores, make sure Jacob was sufficiently hydrated and check for constipation and/or abdominal issues. Simone made delicious homemade soups and some tasty casseroles that they were able to mince up for easy consumption. With medication, they were able to keep the pain under control. Surprisingly, Jacob was in good spirits. He had some visitors from the seniors' centre and James came twice a week for a visit and to give Janet a break.

"How are you, Gramps?" James would come in and sit on the bed.

"Ah, not bad for an old man dying" was always the standard reply.

They would play checkers or James would read to him. Jacob was enjoying the Harry Potter series and he would ask Janet or James to read to him. James enjoyed this because he got to read the stories as well. He wasn't much of a reader before. On his latest visit, James told Jacob about how he was going to see his mom soon.

"How do you feel about that?" Jacob asked.

"Not sure, really. I think she is ready to come home now, but she wants to see me first before coming back. It's going to be strange; it's been just me and Dad for so long."

"You are a good boy; you have been through so much for one so young."

"Thanks, Gramps. I am going miss you . . ." James lowered his face so that Jacob wouldn't see the tears in his eyes.

"Promise me you will keep in touch with Janet. She is going to need you after I am gone."

"Sure thing." They sat quietly for a bit.

"When was the last time you saw the vision, Jacob?" James asked.

"Ooh, a while, that's for sure."

"Do you want to go and see her?"

"How can we do that?"

"We have got the wheelchair and Janet could drive right to the spot and let us out. With the two of us, I'm sure we could take you there."

Jacob thought about it for a moment. "I know it may be difficult, but while I'm feeling pretty good, why not? . . . Yes, why not?" Jacob laughed and his eyes twinkled with mischief.

When Janet got back from her break, they confronted her with their plan.

"Oh Jacob, what if something happens?" Janet said, concerned.

"Something is going to happen—that's why I want to do it now."

Janet looked from Jacob to James and knew their minds were made up.

"Okay, against my better judgement, you understand."

James high-fived Jacob and they put their plan into action.

It was easy enough to get Jacob into the car. They folded up the wheelchair and put it in the trunk. When they got to the spot where the path was, James pulled out the wheelchair and, with Janet's help, got Jacob into it. Janet went off to park and the two waited for her to come back. The path was not even or concreted, so it was a bumpy ride. They got stuck in some holes but managed to pull the wheelchair out of them. They finally reached the altar and both Janet and Jacob were sweating from their excursion.

"I think we should leave you alone with Mary," Janet said, breathless. James and Janet left Jacob to sit with his own thoughts in front of the altar. He looked up and smiled. "They certainly have looked after me well, Mary.

I want to thank you for bringing us together. We needed one another and you gave us that chance to get to know one another and become friends. I am so glad you gave an old codger like me a second chance." Jacob smelled the familiar perfume and saw the light come up. There she was in all her glory. Jacob basked in her beauty and light. He asked that she look after Janet and James when he was gone. The light faded and once again, he was alone.

"Thank you, Mary, thank you so much."

Chapter 48

James

James was busy clearing tables. It was Friday evening and the place was hopping. He was jumping from dishwashing to clearing tables. He was about to go into the kitchen, when he heard a familiar voice.

He turned around and saw Lisa. She was with a guy, probably from her grade, as James didn't recognize him. She was trying to get James' attention and when he looked at her, she smiled. James didn't know what to think. Was she purposely being a bitch to flaunt this new guy in his face, or what? James stomped into the kitchen. He began slamming pots and pans around, jamming dishes into the dishwasher. "Hey, you gonna break something," one of the chefs scolded. "What's got into you?"

James muttered, "Nothing," but was more careful with the dishes. James was asked to go out and clear some tables soon after that. He deliberately didn't look at Lisa. He quickly cleared and went back into the kitchen. He heard one of the waiters, Barry, talking to someone outside the kitchen door. "Can't you wait until he is finished his shift?" James stopped what he was doing and heard Lisa's voice, but he couldn't hear what she was saying. "Okay, but only a couple of minutes, it's busy in here." The kitchen door opened and Lisa came in.

"Hi, James." She walked up to him. James ushered her towards the back door and they went outside.

"What's going on?" he asked her accusingly.

"I had to see you, I had to explain." She put her hand on his arm and he pulled it away.

"I wasn't allowed to see you and I didn't feel I should go to the funeral. I'm sorry, sorry for everything."

"Who's the guy?" James motioned towards the restaurant.

"He's just a friend. I found out you were working here and I asked him to bring me here, so I could see you."

"James!" someone shouted from the kitchen.

"Look I have to go. I will call you if that's what you want."

"Yes, I would like that." They walked back through the kitchen and Lisa went into the restaurant.

"Someone's got it bad." Paul, the sous-chef wolf whistled.

"Shut up, Paul." James gave him the finger but was laughing as he did it. The rest of the night was gags about James and Lisa, but James took it in his stride. He couldn't believe Lisa came here to see him. When his shift finished, James rode his bike home as quickly as he could. Even though it was late, he texted Lisa. She responded straight away. They texted back and forth for a while and agreed to meet up for a walk tomorrow. James hit the pillow and for the first time in a long time had sweet dreams that night.

Chapter 49

Janet

Janet was kept busy looking after Jacob. She catered to his every need. He was an easy patient and was happiest when either she, James or Simone sat quietly with him or read to him. Janet didn't want to dwell on what was going to happen when Jacob had to go to a hospice. She wanted to keep him here as long as possible.

Jacob was having a nap when Janet got the mail from the letterbox located outside the front door. There were a few bills for Jacob and a letter addressed to her. The postmark was from Ontario, but there was no return address. It was addressed to her previous apartment. Janet tore open the envelope. It was a letter from her adoptive father. It read:

Dear Janet,

Hope this finds you well. I sincerely hope you get this letter, as I don't have a new address for you but, knowing how efficient you are, I am sure you will have your mail redirected. I am not sure if you want to hear from me but I have to do this for my own sake. I wish things could have been different. I wish I had not taken that job in Ontario and left you behind. I should have insisted that you come with us or not accepted the job. Anyway, what is done is done, and we can't erase the past, but I want to make amends in the future.

Just to let you know that your brother's wedding was big, expensive and, I have to say it, pretentious. Your mother loved it!!! Dare I say more? I hope that they find happiness together, but I have a feeling it won't last long. You did the right thing by not coming. I know you struggle with anxiety and some other phobias that I don't understand, but I am going to make an effort to be compassionate about them. I want to ask a favour of you. I have no idea where you are living or what you are doing, but I would like to come and visit for a while. I am being selfish here. I need to see you. Your mother and I are struggling with our relationship and we need some time apart, but mostly I want to see you and try to make up for all the times I wasn't there for you. I didn't know your mother was going to see you and she only told me about how she threw you out of your apartment after it was too late to do anything. The thing is, I am a coward. I have let your mother bully me for a long time. I was willing for her to call all the shots but when I realized I would lose you, I couldn't do it anymore. I understand that you are going to contact your biological mother. I think that is great. We all need a second chance and I am hoping you will give me one as well. Please let me know what you think, even if you don't want to see me again.

P.S. Sorry for the scribble, I wanted to write this by hand. Hope you can read my chicken scratch.

Love, your dad.

After his sign-off he had included a number for Janet to call him collect. She immediately got up and dialled the number. She quickly calculated the time difference and it was about 4:00 p.m. in the afternoon where her father was. He answered after three rings.

"Dad it's me . . . Janet. I got your letter . . ." Janet spoke with her dad for over an hour. She would pay Jacob for the call. (Her dad said he would but she declined his offer.) She told him all about Jacob and where she was living and what she was doing. She told him about the meeting she had with Irene and they both cried on the phone. Janet said she would definitely have him to visit but he would have to wait. She would not be able to give her full attention to Jacob if her dad was here. Her father understood and would wait until the timing was right. He said he would call next week and, if it was okay with her, call on a weekly basis.

"Yes, please. It has been so wonderful to speak with you. Thank you so much."

"I love you, Janet, I hope you know that. Despite my bad behaviour, I have always loved you."

"I love you too, Dad. Talk to you next week." Janet hung up the phone. She had another call to make.

When James came by the next day to see Jacob, Janet went to the mall and called Irene from the pay phone. Janet was thankful that she answered.

"Janet, honey, I am so glad you called. I was afraid you weren't going to see me again."

Janet explained that she was looking after a friend and that it was too difficult to see her at this time, but she would be in touch and arrange a meeting as soon as she was able.

"I appreciate that, thank you. Good luck with your friend."

Janet did not go into the details of Jacob's illness and the fact that he was dying.

"I will talk to you soon." Janet hesitated but then said, "Can I ask you, Irene, what happened that made you go onto the street?" There was a pause and then Irene said, "There were a number of things but the main one was not having good parents. That sounds like I'm being hypocritical after having to give you up, but it's true. They just didn't care about me. They were drug addicts and their next fix was more important than their child. I fell through the system and wasn't taken care of, so I had to look after myself, which I did for the most part. I left home when I was 15. Like I said before, the streets were a lot better than some other places I lived at. I want you to know, I didn't prostitute or take drugs. I do have values, I really do. It has taken me a long time to get where I am now, but I did it and I did it on my own." Janet could hear the pride in Irene's voice.

"Thank you for telling me and I do want to find out more about you. I sincerely mean that."

"I have lots of stories . . ." Irene laughed

"Well, I will be in touch, take care, bye." Janet hung up the phone. She felt a huge relief wash over her. Their meetings would be on her terms but they would be meeting again, which she knew in her heart she wanted to do. Janet also felt she had some of Irene's fortitude, like making it on her own and achieving something, even though it was often difficult.

Janet went home and told James and Jacob all about her dad contacting her and her phone call with Irene.

Chapter 50

Jacob

Jacob could see Lorraine in the distance; she started walking closer and closer to him. She held her hand out to him. "It's time, Jacob, it's time to come home." Jacob woke up with a start. He had been dreaming. He felt his bedclothes and his face and knew he was still living. After that dream, though, Jacob knew his time on this earth was limited. He called out to Janet to come in and see him.

"Jacob, what can I get for you?" Janet sat on the bed and smiled at Jacob.

"It is time for me to go to the hospice."

"Why, are you in pain?" Janet looked alarmed.

"No, I actually feel pretty good, but that's the point. I don't want to be taken to hospital when things start to go bad. I would like to end my days at a pleasant place and it would be better for you. I want you to remember this house as a place of living and fun, not of disease and dying." Janet couldn't say anything—she was too choked up. She kissed his whiskered face. Janet gently closed the bedroom door and called to make the arrangements.

Jacob went into the hospice the following week. It was a beautiful place, with a garden, family room and chapel. It had all the amenities of a home, where staff and family could go to a kitchen and make drinks and use the fridge. There was a television in each room but also a television room where residents could sit and watch TV with others. They also had a lovely meditation room, which was used for silent contemplation. There were healers that came in, to do therapeutic touch and massage, as well as pets that came to visit. Volunteers were there to talk to or to get drinks and light snacks. There was even an in-house laundry facility. Jacob had a lovely room facing the garden. There were huge red rhododendrons outside his window and a humming bird feeder attached to a small tree. He loved to watch the little birds buzz around and taste the sweet syrup. Just after he started to settle in, Jacob took a turn for the worse. His deterioration was rapid. He was kept as comfortable as possible and was in and out of consciousness for three days. Janet never left his side. She was able to get a cot bed put in his room. She didn't really sleep. She was by his side for every gasp or shudder he made. James came in to see him but understandably he couldn't stay for the end. Simone wept openly by his side, not able to hold anything back. Janet comforted her.

Jacob took his last breath early Friday morning. He opened his eyes briefly and squeezed Janet's hand. He then slumped forward and everything was still. Janet placed him back on his pillows and thankfully his eyes were closed. She kissed his forehead, tears streaming down her face, not bothering to brush them away. She stood by the window and looked out. She saw a humming bird come to the feeder. It buzzed around and then flew right up to the window. It stayed there for a long time. Janet smiled. She knew it was a sign from Jacob. He was happy now and free. "Good-bye, my sweet man. I am going to miss you." Janet then went to the nurse to let her know.

They had an intimate gathering of people at the seniors' centre to celebrate Jacob's life. All of the seniors he had connected with were there, as well as Simone and, of course, Janet and James. Janet called Jacob's brother in Florida but he wasn't able to come up. He was recovering from heart surgery and couldn't travel. Despite finding out his brother had just died, he was very distant. Janet gathered that the brothers were not that close.

They had some of Jacob's favourite music and some of Simone's signature sandwiches and cakes. Janet got up to make a speech. "I just want to thank all of you for coming out to celebrate Jacob's life. I know at times he was difficult and, for a long time, he was bitter. He had lost his precious Lorraine and he felt life was not worth living. Jacob found solace in little things, like his crosswords, certain TV programs, the park, and the few friends he let into his life. He found peace in his spirituality near the end. He was able to draw upon the Grace of a celestial being that put him back firmly amongst the living, and when he got sick, it made it easier for him to leave this earth. I feel blessed to have known him and he will always be there . . ." Janet found it difficult to compose herself, but she did: ". . . always in my heart." She sat down, and she and James hugged one another. Simone gently put her hand on her shoulders. The small crowd applauded, and Simone said in a strong voice, "Let's eat."

Jacob was cremated by request and the ashes were held in a gold urn. Just after Jacob was diagnosed with colon cancer, he went to his lawyer and had his will amended. He left the townhouse to Janet and a large sum of money to Simone. He also put some money in trust for James to use for either his education or for travelling, when he reached 20. They were all touched by his generosity and love.

One early Saturday morning, Janet and James walked from the nearby street where she parked her car. They had the urn with them and were going to spread the ashes. They walked to the path they had all been on so many times that year and made their way to the altar. They both bowed their heads in their own prayers. Janet came forward and placed the urn on the altar. She turned around to face James and spoke. "This place has become a safe haven for all of us and it seems fitting that we spread Jacob's ashes here. Whenever we come to visit Mary, we can remember Jacob as well."

Janet stepped back and James came forward. "It has been tough for all of us but I wouldn't be in the space I am today"—James touched his heart and head,—"without Mary; you, Janet; and Jacob. I feel like I have known all of you all my life and you are all very special to me. Thank you . . ."

Janet came forward and held James' hand. Together they opened the urn and spread the ashes all around the altar. They stepped back and, still holding hands, bowed their heads. The wind picked up and, with it, the ashes. They swirled, danced and shot up in the air. The ashes then deposited themselves all around the site. Nothing happened at first and James and Janet were about to leave when, suddenly, the dazzling light came into view. Mary appeared before them. She wasn't alone, though. On one side of her was Diana, James' sister, and on the other side was Jacob. Diana was strong and well; Jacob was robust and standing without his cane. They all looked peaceful and content. Janet and James looked at one another in recognition of what they both were seeing. Jacob gave a cocky salute and Diana blew a kiss. Mary had her signature smile of love that radiated out to them. The light faded and they were gone. Janet and James couldn't have asked for a better send-off for their beloved friend. They walked back to the car in silence. They had a date at the coffee shop.

Chapter 51

James and Janet

Janet and James sat in their usual spot, having their drinks as normal, with the only exception being that their friend was missing. They pulled up the third chair anyway. Based on what they had just seen, he was there in spirit. Janet put her drink down and looked at James. He had grown in height these past few months. He was an attractive young man. There was sadness in the eyes, though, which she hoped would fade with time. Irene had said that she had sad eyes. They both needed time; time to heal, time to grow and time to move on.

"So I understand you saw your mother?

"Yeah, she has actually come back home."

"How is it?"

"Hard. We are avoiding each other, not like before, but because we don't know what to say to one another. We are going to start counselling together as a family and then I still see Greg." James thought for a moment and his face lit up. "Hey, you should meet him. You would really like him, and I know he would like you too."

"Don't start any matchmaking ideas, not yet anyway. I have some things I need to sort out myself."

James laughed. "So when does your dad arrive?"

"He is coming on Monday. I am really looking forward to it. Just like you need to start over with your mom, I need to start over with my dad. It's going to be strange . . . and then I am meeting up with Irene. I might even bring my dad along. Who knows? So what's happening with Lisa?"

"We are seeing one another again, but I'm not sure how it will go. She's nice and everything, but I don't want to rush into some kind of heavy relationship."

"Listen to the wise one, here. You're right, though—you are too young to be getting serious." Janet changed the subject. "I start my course in two weeks and I guess you are going into grade 11—wow!"

"Yeah, kind of scary but I'm looking forward to it. I never really liked school, but this last year, I was really stoked that I passed all my subjects and now I even want to do well in them. Crazy, huh? I hope to get on the track team as well. I love running; it makes me feel good."

James stopped for a minute. He looked embarrassed but carried on. "We are still going to meet up every Saturday, I hope. I really like talking to you and you're kind of like a, well, sister to me."

Janet impulsively hugged James. "Of course we will. I need to see and talk to you as well. You *are* my little brother." James was pleased that she had said that.

"Will you still go to see the vision?" Janet asked

"Oh yeah, I know she is there whenever I need her."

"Good, I plan to do the same." They sat in silence for bit. Janice finished her drink. "Well, I better get back and start to clean my house, get ready for when my dad comes." Janet loved it when she said "my house." It was still very much Jacob's house too—she could feel his presence everywhere.

"What is Simone going to do now?" James asked.

"She is still working but she comes and gives me cooking lessons every week. Really, it is just an excuse for us to see one another. I can't wait for my dad to meet her, especially when she cooks him a meal. He will love that."

They walked out of the coffee shop. James said he was meeting Lisa, so they parted ways with a promise to see one another next Saturday.

Epilogue

The vision of Mother Mary brought together three people in need, in need of one another and in need of some deeper spiritual "mentor"—someone they could turn to and call upon when life became too much for them. The vision was still there for Janet and James. Now three more people's lives would become intertwined with each other and the vision.

Lin-Lin was finding it difficult to settle in to her new surroundings. She was a new ESL student from China. She had been brought over by her aunt who felt she would be better off here to learn English. She missed her family in Beijing. She knew she should be honoured to come here, but she couldn't help but feel unhappy. Lin-Lin liked to walk through the park; it made her feel better. She loved the large trees and all the flowers, particularly the roses in the rose garden. Lin-Lin needed to practise her verbs before going to class. The English language was so difficult to master. She sighed. She noticed a path off to the side. She decided to explore it . . .

Andy had all his possessions in his shopping cart. He would travel around with it on the streets during the day, but he wanted to find a new place to sleep at night. He liked walking through the park; even with all the animals, he felt safer there somehow. It was becoming too dangerous on the downtown eastside. Other people stealing his stuff when he slept, junkies fighting, storekeepers telling him to move on and not being nice about it either. He had found a new area where he liked to sit and eat his food. There was an altar there. He didn't know why but it made him feel at ease. Maybe he could set up camp here to sleep.

Moira loved to go out after "work" with an absolutely clear face. She would scrub every bit of makeup off and exfoliate her skin. She was very particular with her regimen of cleaning. She had beautiful skin, everyone told her that. She didn't really need makeup, but she used it for her work. It was like putting on a mask. She could be someone else with the makeup and the tight clothes and high heels and then Moira would transform into "Misty," the stripper. Now she was just Moira with her regular jeans, a plain oversized t-shirt and her flat shoes. Moira liked to walk along the seawall; it was good exercise and she enjoyed the fresh sea air. She would take great gulps of it, to banish the stinky, sweaty, stale air of the strip joints. Moira went by the lagoon to see the ducks. They were comical to her—the way they went upside down in the water made her smile. She didn't smile much, because she didn't have a lot to smile about. She noticed a path off the main walkway. For some reason, she felt intrigued by it. She wanted to follow it to see where it led . . .

CPSIA information can be obtained at www.ICGtesting.com
Printed in the USA
LVOW131522120113

315413LV00004B/76/P